WAITING FOR JUNE

WAITING FOR JUNE

FOR

JUNE

BY JOYCE SWEENEY

Marshall Cavendish

Text copyright © 2003 by Joyce Sweeney
All rights reserved
Marshall Cavendish, 99 White Plains Road, Tarrytown, NY 10591
www.marshallcavendish.us

Library of Congress Cataloging-in-Publication Data
Sweeney, Joyce.
Waiting for June / by Joyce Sweeney.
p. cm.
Summary: In the third trimester of her pregnancy, Florida high school senior Sophie tries to
discover the identity of the father she has never known, while adamantly refusing to disclose the
name of her own baby's father.
ISBN-13: 978-0-7614-5329-1 (paperback)
ISBN-10: 0-7614-5329-6 (paperback)
ISBN-10: 0-7614-5138 (hardcover)
[1. Pregnancy—Fiction. 2. Friendship—Fiction. 3. High schools—Fiction. 4. Schools—Fiction.
5. Racially mixed people—Fiction. 6. Mothers and daughters—Fiction.] I. Title.
PZ7.S97427Wa 2003
[Fic]—dc21
2002156711

The text of this book is set in 11-point Jansen.
Original hardcover book design by Anahid Hamparian

Printed in the United States of America

First Marshall Cavendish paperback edition, 2006

2 4 6 5 3 1

ITC Marshall Cavendish

ACKNOWLEDGMENTS

Thanks to my readers: Jay Sweeney, Heidi Boehringer, Joan Mazza and Alexandra Flinn. Thanks to George Nicholson, for guiding me through rough waters, and Margery Cuyler, for giving me safe harbor. Special thanks to my Thursday Group—your excellence in writing has raised the bar for me.

To Margery Cuyler, with gratitude, respect and affection

WAiTiNG FOR JUNE

I'm in my third trimester now, when dreams are supposed to be especially vivid. Lately, I've been dreaming about whales, pale and bloated, drifting in a murky sea.

They're always at the edge of my visual horizon, sometimes moving out of sight, which panics me. I don't know if I'm supposed to be human or another whale, left behind by the pod, but it seems important to catch up, and I never do.

The memorable part of this dream is the sound, the whale songs that roll over me in the water, so my body feels the sound and knows its shape.

The whales cry in pulses, the most comforting sequence of beats imaginable. Not fast, like a heartbeat. Not even the pace of breathing. Slow. Like the rhythm of someone stroking a cat.

My senior counselor, Mrs. Treadmore, says the sonogram brought on this dream. She points out that whales communicate with ultrasound, and that in the beginning the fetus is like a fish.

"But a whale isn't a fish," I tell her. "It's a cetacean mammal."

"Even so," she says, tapping her hard nails on the edge of her desk. She always says "even so" when I try to disagree with her. It's the adult version of "whatever—."

As she talks to me, her fingers sneak up to the telephone on her desk and tap the buttons. Her hands are impatient with me, ready to go on to the next task. But she thinks she has to be careful with me or I'll drop out of school or kill myself or both. Mrs. Treadmore expects me to be depressed, but I love my baby. I know from the sonogram she's a girl. She's been sending me the dreams. I think she knows some kind of magic and wants to share it with me.

She already knows I can be trusted with secrets.

We sit in assembly, trying not to die of boredom. Joshua has a toy, a fuzzy purple chick from his little sister's Easter basket. If you cup it in your hand the right way, it makes a soft peeping sound. Just loud enough to disturb the kids around us but not loud enough to get us in trouble. Joshua and I always sit in the back of assembly. Mostly so the kids who hate our friendship will have to turn all the way around if they want to glower. Everyone thinks Joshua is the father of my baby; and since he's African American, and even more important, popular, it means no one thinks I have any business being anywhere near him.

Ms. Rowling, our principal, is telling us about the Nestor Chanate gym and how it will be dedicated at a special ceremony next month. We've all done about ten million service projects to help raise money for the gym. Everyone was glad to. Nobody wants to play in the old gym anymore. All you can see is Nestor jumping up to the basket and folding in the air like a jackknife, crashing to the ground and getting stepped on by his teammates, who, like all of us, couldn't believe a seventeen-year-old athlete could have a heart attack and die just like that.

When Joshua gets nervous, he acts silly. Now he leans forward and puts the chick on Acacia Williams's shoulder. She has already turned around several times to shush him and tell him he's immature. I guess they like each other, which automatically makes her dislike me. The chick tumbles into her lap, and she turns around. Her angry eyes are like stars. "Stop it!" she whispers and shows him she is confiscating the chick. She snaps it into her green lizardy purse. Acacia always has nice things. I wish she would take me shopping and show me her secrets.

Joshua leans forward, huge hands dangling between his knees. His whisper ruffles the edge of Acacia's hair. "Hey! Give me that back! That's my pet!"

A laugh makes her shoulder spasm, but she refuses to turn around.

"My little pet chicken!" Joshua laments. "Named . . . Brucie."

Now her shoulders jiggle up and down. Joshua is hard to resist.

"Oh, Brucie," he whispers. "My little Brucie, can you breathe inside there, honey? Are you choking in there with all that lip gloss and those credit cards?"

A musical giggle erupts from Acacia. Lots of people turn around.

"In the back?" Ms. Rowlings calls through the microphone.

It's enough of a threat. Joshua sits back in his seat. After a second, Acacia opens her purse and quietly passes back the chick.

Everyone turns and frowns. At me.

Joshua walks me home from school. I never had many friends before I got pregnant, but now it's just down to Joshua. Brucie is long gone, got trampled in fifth period.

Joshua hopes his sister won't notice, but she will. Kimberly notices everything.

"Want me to stop here?" he asks two blocks short of my house.

"No!" I snap at him, even though I'm angry at my mother. She'd do anything to get Joshua out of my life.

"You shouldn't take up with her," he scolds me. "It stresses the baby."

I walk faster. He's making me mad. He doesn't know what's going on inside me. He catches my arm, gently pulls me to a stop. "Does she have a name yet?" he asks.

This is his way of apologizing, of showing me he knows it's my baby and I'm the authority. "No," I say. "I think she's trying to tell me her name, but I can't hear it yet."

I wouldn't say that to anyone else, but Joshua just smiles and says, "Cool." He has a beautiful smile. It's no wonder girls fall all over themselves trying to get a date with him.

For a minute I just want to stand there, looking at Joshua's smile, before I have to go into my house. Somehow he knows this and goes with it. I listen to the birds warbling in the trees around us, watch the breeze blow a stream of yellow pollen along the sidewalk. How can people say there are no seasons in Florida? Are they blind?

Joshua just stands there patiently, knowing he's not supposed to talk. I close my eyes and breathe and feel something balance inside me.

When I turn to walk on, he's right in step.

My mother is ironing washcloths in the dark. The living room is like a cave after the March sunshine. All the verticals are snapped shut.

Steam seems to rise from my mother's hands as she presses the point hard into the terry cloth. She makes a fold and mashes the creases. In her short-sleeved top, her elbow looks sharp, like a weapon.

My mother doesn't look like me. Her face has always looked foreign to me: small, sunken eyes, pointed chin, blonde hair that won't hold a curl. My hair is brown and hangs in wild curls, and my eyes are green. Photographed together, we look like beings from two different planets.

"Hi," I say. Every day I fake a cheerful greeting, hoping like a fool to make a fresh start.

She props up the iron, and it hisses. "Did you walk home with that boy again?"

She doesn't mean "boy" in the racist way. I don't think . . . "Joshua," I correct her. "He has a name."

She looks down. Presses the cloth she's already pressed. "Why does he want to hang around you, Sophie?" she says. "Do you ever ask yourself that?"

I jerk the cord on the verticals, blasting her with sunshine. "Maybe I'm a likable person!" Here comes the edge in my voice. I hate these fights, but they always happen. I can't seem to control myself around her.

Her hand flies up like a visor. "Please close that!" she wails, like I've hit her.

I snap it shut so hard, the plastic strips dance like skeletons. "What are you?" I shout. "A vampire?"

Once she has me upset, she always gets very calm. "It fades the upholstery. The Florida sun is too strong. You don't have to think of things like that because you have no responsibilities. When the baby comes, everything will change."

I'm frozen with fear at these words. What if it's true? Maybe before I was born she was a normal person who didn't fear the sun or the wrinkles in a washcloth. The day I told her I was pregnant, when she was done crying, she said, "Well, you can forget about being a writer now."

When I was little, we were so happy.

"All we need is each other," she used to say. When I came home from school, I might find a picnic spread on the living-room floor or a treasure hunt set up with real clues that led to a Hershey bar tucked between the sofa cushions. "I may not have anything else in this world," she often said, "but I have you."

Thinking of this, I realize it wasn't my birth that destroyed her—it was something about my growing up. Every milestone seemed to make her angrier. My first period, my first day of high school, my friendship with Joshua, and the absolute, crowning glory: my pregnancy. Somehow I broke a promise to her I never made.

Each year the house got a little darker: the tasks she set for herself got a little more demanding. She stopped going out, except to work. She even stopped eating real food. She just drinks Slim Fast, not to lose weight but because it keeps her alive with the least amount of effort.

Maybe I got pregnant for her, thinking a new baby would make her happy again. But I was certainly wrong.

Now I want to fight. "Is the washcloth inspector coming?" I ask her.

"I hope," she says calmly, "that when you have a home of your own, you'll have some standards, too." She has finished the last washcloth. She looks around the room hungrily for something else to press.

"Why don't we go out to dinner?" I plead. "Maybe we could have some fun."

"Fun!" She jerks the iron cord out of the wall. "I guess that's how you got in this mess you're in in the first place."

Like a volcano, my voice explodes out in a scream. "My baby is not a mess!" I go to my room and slam the door.

Joshua's right about me. I waste my energy on all the wrong things.

☆

By five o'clock I'm starving but too proud to go out for a snack, so I concoct snacks in my head. A grilled cheese sandwich slathered in butter and Lowrys garlic salt. A glass of milk with half a can of Hershey's syrup poured in.

We're supposed to write poems for English tomorrow. A chore for everyone else, but I breathe poems. English teachers love me, and sometimes it's mutual, like this year with Mr. Kissanis. He's the best teacher I've ever had. So good, you wonder what crime he committed that he has to teach high school instead of being a professor at a university. He has us reading Edith Hamilton's Mythology because he's Greek, and he says the Greeks wrote the stories everyone's been imitating ever since.

We're supposed to pick our favorite myth and write a poem about it. I know I will write about Persephone because when we did it in class, I didn't get to say everything I wanted to say. The story is, Persephone was out picking flowers, and Hades, the god of the underworld, made the ground open up and swallow her. He wanted to make her his bride. But then her mother, Demeter, who I guess is in charge of corn, got really mad and sued for custody; and the way they settled it was that Persephone was with her mother part of the time when the flowers are blooming up here and part of the time—winter—with Hades.

In class everyone, Mr. Kissanis included, kept acting like, poor Persephone, married to the god of the dead and can only be up here part of the time. Poor little thing.

But if you read the myth, you see it doesn't really say that much about what Persephone thought. Hades gave her pomegranate seeds that made her want to stay in the underworld. It was her mother who wanted everything back like it was. If I had a choice, right now, of being in the underworld with a guy who really wanted me versus planting corn with my mother, you can believe I'd be down there scarfing the pomegranates.

So that's what I want my poem to be about.

I open my journal (about the twentieth in a series), go to a clean page, and give it a try.

Open, earth, and swallow

The rhyming word "follow" pops in my head.

Open, earth, and swallow, follow

Follow what? What would it be like? I loved the idea of her going down in a fissure like that. You would see the strata of the rocks and the roots of the plants.

Open earth and swallow, follow
rootlines of her flowers
lower, lower
down to where

It would be dark in this world. But not dark like my living room in the middle of the afternoon. Dark like when a boy kisses you, and you close your eyes.

down to where
all senses are useless
but touch

I may keep this poem for myself. I'm not sure I want Mr. Kissanis to read it. But for now I'll just try to finish it and then decide. I can always knock off something about Narcissus and Echo if this one gets too heavy.

My baby is shifting around. She hates it when I sit up at a desk or a table. I slide around in my seat until she feels like she's happy again.

Hades, Hades. He's not the devil or anything. We studied him. He's Zeus's brother. The brothers divided up the world, and he got everything under the ground. He cleverly got the mineral rights, Mr. Kissanis said, and ended up very rich. But he had to be in charge of the place for dead people, which again, the way the Greeks describe it, isn't like hell or anything. It's just sort of a shadowy, vague place with these pale flowers. Like a dreamworld, I keep thinking. Hades had a hat that made him invisible, and Hermes, the messenger god, got it later. Hermes seemed to end up with everyone's best stuff.

> *The invisible man*
> *is waiting*
> *Forbidden fruit in his hands*
> *The roses above wilt*
> *The ground below*

I need a verb. I want to say the ground below does something, goes crazy, blooms like crazy, with asphodel. That's the name of those pale flowers. I try word after word. Swells, explodes, erupts, blooms, blossoms, flowers.

I can't get it. My baby kicks me. "What?" I say. "Do you know the word?" I put my hand over her, so she knows I'm paying attention. Last week there was a little spotting, but the doctor checked me out and said it was okay.

Bleeds. A perfect word. I recopy my poem in its perfect form.

> *Persephone*
>
> *Open earth, and swallow, follow*
> *rootlines of her flowers*
> *lower, lower*
> *down to where*
> *all senses are useless*
> *but touch*
>
> *The invisible man*
> *is waiting*
> *Forbidden fruit in his hands*

9

The roses above wilt
The ground below bleeds asphodel

I like it a lot as I read it over, and I decide I have to turn it in, because it's one of my best poems ever, and I want the credit. Anyway, I'm eighteen and pregnant, so what am I supposed to write about, bunnies and daffodils?

A few months ago, I tried to make a deal with my mother. I told her I'd tell her who the baby's father was, if she'd tell me about my father.

Her answer was, "You don't want to know."

That night the whales come again. I'm standing in some kind of circular inlet or bay. Behind me the sun is setting and the sky is orange, but the water in front of me is already dark and the air is cooling.

Out beyond the breakers I see whales jumping and slapping the water with their tails. I know they are calling to me.

I start to walk into the surf. It's warm compared to the air, and I taste salt. I walk deeper and deeper, bracing myself every few seconds as a wave breaks over me. Then I begin to swim.

Under the surface everything is murky and chartreuse. I can feel the whales around me, and then I can see them. They seem to stare at me, then they swim away a few feet and circle back. They want me to follow them.

The water feels so good to my skin, I can't even explain it with waking words. After a while, I don't use my arms anymore; I just ripple my body up and down like they do. My legs are together, like a fluke. We swim in formation, and every few minutes we all surface to breathe together. Each time we come up, I get a glimpse of the moon.

I realize they have turned me into a whale, or I have turned myself into a whale. We are in very deep water now, and I wonder how I'll ever get back, but I love being with them. I know I have passed a test, and they have accepted me.

We all hover in the water, and they sing to me. They repeat the same syllables over and over, and I struggle to join in; but I don't know how to make the sounds.

I open my mouth and try to shout the magic syllables, after something explodes in the water and puts me back in my bed, my nightgown soaked with sweat, my stomach rolling with nausea.

I sit up on the edge of the bed. "Damn it," I say to my baby. "They were trying to tell me your name!"

2

Debbie Treadmore has a new idea today. Vocational school. I mess up the interview right from the start by laughing.

"I'm already enrolled for the fall at Broward Community College," I explain as her glare hardens over me like doughnut glaze. "I'm going to get a B.A. in English."

"And where," she asks, "will your daughter be while you're pursuing the liberal arts? Are you planning to burden your mother with the responsibility?"

"I don't burden my mother," I say, and pause while I add in my head, *My mother burdens me.* "I'm planning to move out and get an apartment and a job this summer. I've been saving money since I was a freshman. I think if you look at the file, you'll see I already got an academic scholarship and a Pell grant and a student loan."

"Which you will pay back as soon as you start working as a poet." She snorts. She fiddles with the things on her desk, a sure sign she's getting mad. Her fingers toy with a letter opener.

I sit back in my chair, feeling every aching muscle from

my shoulders to my pelvis. She doesn't want me to succeed, I think. And then I see she's like my mother—trying patiently to get me to feel how doomed I'm supposed to be.

How can I explain to her what I've already learned about life? That if you just throw yourself in the direction you want to go, something always catches you. If I tried to talk about this, she wouldn't even hear me.

"Maybe we should stop having these sessions," I say.

I hear her think the word, *surly*. My baby is making me a little psychic, too. Mrs. Treadmore's nails drum the desk like galloping hooves. "Do you want another counselor, Sophie?"

This time I manage to hold the laugh in as I think of Ms. Cellini, who calls high school students "Sweetie" and "Honey" and always ends up telling you her problems. Or maybe Mr. Lechter, Joshua's counselor, who cleans his ears with his car keys and asked Joshua once if he felt like "rapping." Joshua, being Joshua, said, "Sure," stood up, and sang the chorus of "Gangsta's Paradise," complete with gestures.

"I don't think I need counseling," I say carefully. "Because I know what I'm going to do, and I have confidence in myself, and I'm very happy."

You'd think that would make a counselor happy, wouldn't you? But Debbie Treadmore narrows her eyes until she seems to be nothing but eyeliner. "May I ask you a question?" she says.

I sigh. "I guess."

"Are you including the baby's father in any of these well-laid plans?"

I wait for a moment of almost nuclear anger to pass. "No."

Tap, tap. "Do you think that's fair?"

I compress my mouth so that only clean words can get out. "I think it's the only thing that makes sense." She wants me to say who the father is, of course. Like the whole rest of the world.

"Don't you suppose he has some feelings in the matter?" she asks.

I tell the truth. "I don't know if he does or not."

She unintentionally looks at my breasts and frowns. Behind her back a lot of the boys call her "Surfboard." "Sophie, I just hope you don't end up with a lot of regrets." She pushes her chair back, which means "beat it."

I get up slowly, gather my books and water bottle. "You, too" is all I can think of to say.

Mr. Kissanis is a gorgeous man. They call him "Yanni" because of his moustache and his brown ponytail; but he's bigger, younger, and handsomer than that. When someone stands in front of you for an hour every day, you start noticing their body. His body is worth noticing. He's married and has something like fourteen kids, I hear. Today he wears a linen shirt the color of vanilla ice cream.

I'm sitting back on my spine this period because my baby is trying to swim around in my stomach and this is the only position that works. I have on my jeans—can't give them up, but now I have a big safety pin in the front as an extender. Over that I have a big, pink cotton shirt. My hair is draped over the back of the chair to get it off my neck.

"What is a good poem?" Mr. Kissanis asks us as he paces around the room. "Put your hands down. Put your hands down. You don't know. There are no definitions for poetry, or art or feelings . . . Maybe everything that's worthwhile in life defies explanation."

I struggle to sit up. I want to write that down.

"Nobody can say what love is." He gives us a sly sideways look. "But you all know it if you feel it. The same is true of a good poem. You don't have to know what it's about to feel it."

He circles to his desk and picks up a sheet of turquoise notebook paper. I realize it's my poem, and he's going to read it out loud. My Persephone poem. I put both hands on my stomach to hold my baby still. I don't know what I'm feeling.

"'Open, earth, and swallow,'" he reads.

Someone giggles. I go stiff.

"'Follow rootlines of her flowers. Lower, lower.'"

I hear a whisper behind me, but I can't make it out.

He's oblivious, in love with my poem. He walks up and down. "'Down to where all senses are useless but touch.'"

"Whoooo!" says Greg Peterman.

"Stop it," says Mr. Kissanis. "Don't be juvenile! 'The invisible man is waiting . . . .'" A guy in front of me makes those squiggly fingers, like, Oooh, I'm scared.

"'Forbidden fruit in his hands.'"

A spurt of noise, like a suppressed hoot.

Mr. Kissanis looks angrily in that direction, but on he goes. "'The roses above wilt. The ground below bleeds asphodel.'"

There is a long silence. My face is hot. Still, nobody knows. . . .

"This poem was written by Sophie Cooper," he concludes.

My face burns. My baby lies still, afraid.

"I guess," he plows on, "Mr. Peterman, that if you laugh at a poem like that, it's because mature feelings embarrass you. Sophie is obviously more comfortable with adult themes."

"Obviously!" someone calls. Randy Torres?

Greg Peterman raises his hand. Don't call on him, you idiot!

"Yes?" says Mr. Kissanis.

Greg smiles at me. "I didn't know we could write that kind of poem, Mr. Kissanis. You know, about going down and holding our fruit in our hands and swallowing."

The whole class erupts with laughter. Only then does Mr. Kissanis seem to realize what he's done to me. His eyes rove about the room, amazed at what animals his students are. My paper droops in his hand.

I try to walk fast in the hall, but the baby slows me down. Joshua has basketball practice. I'm all alone.

Greg Peterman, Randy Torres, and Zack Maholic all follow me from perfect earshot distance.

"Hey baby, want to hold my fruit in your hands?"

"Lower, honey, lower."

"Can't she hear me? I must be invisible."

When I was eight years old, I would have turned around and corrected that mixed metaphor. I know better now. It's me who has to become invisible, inaudible, unimportant. They are sharks, and Mr. Kissanis has marked me with blood. All I can do now is move fast and blend, in and maybe they will give up the hunt.

"Do you like to swallow, honey?"

"Nah, if she did, she wouldn't look like she does now!"

I walk faster, elbowing around other kids, almost running. Try to run somewhere with a big tank of water strapped to your middle.

"Sophie, where you going? I want you to write a poem about me."

"Sophie, don't run away. We want you to help us get comfortable with our sexuality. Sophie? Sophie?"

Finally, a girls' bathroom. I push through the door and stand there, panting.

Three girls I only know slightly are in there. One is smoking, one is brushing her hair, one is sitting up on the sink, swinging her feet. They stare at me with pure hatred. But at least their hate is silent.

I go into a stall and vomit.

Reid and I are washed in a soothing, flickering blue light. Reid likes to watch TV in the dark, but his father won't let him. So when I'm babysitting, that's the first thing he wants to do. Reid is in love with TV Land, the world of 1950s sitcoms. *Leave It To Beaver* is just coming on. He's so tranquilized, his mouth is partly open.

I'm on the couch with a bag of my own tranquilizers: sour cream and onion wavy potato chips. Reid's father, Mike, always leaves junk food for me and the baby when I sit. He's my best customer—tips and everything. I have several kids I watch, but Reid is my favorite. He's thirteen now, so my presence is a mere formality; but I think Mike is trying to help me with my college fund, and, since Reid has a crush on me, he's not going to complain if we spend Friday nights together.

"Yes. Yes!" he says. "This is the one where Wally and the Beaver get the baby alligator. Captain Jack."

"Do you want to watch something else?" I tease. "I mean, if you know what's going to happen."

Reid half turns. The blue light emphasizes his long eyelashes, which you don't see in normal light because he's so fair. "It's not the stories; it's the way they live. It's the way all those old-time people lived."

I gently kick him between the shoulder blades with my bare foot. "Oppressing women?"

He turns all the way around, dead serious. "No, Sophie. I didn't mean . . . "

"In the Fifties," I lecture him, "you know what they'd do to me? They'd put me in a home for wayward girls. And they'd take my baby away and give it to a couple in some other town and not tell me where she went. Let's see how many pregnant women we see on Nick at Nite tonight. Even the married ones aren't allowed to show."

"Lucy showed," he says feebly. "Anyway, I'm looking at a whole other thing."

"What?" I ask, because those shows pull me in, too.

He shakes his head. "I don't know how to explain. Everybody's . . . listening when the other person talks. People are . . . concerned about each other."

"It's a fantasy; they probably weren't like that at all," I say. "My baby's moving. You want to feel?"

He gets up with a solemn face, comes over to the couch, and places a chaste hand on the middle of my abdomen, carefully keeping his distance from anything forbidden, either above or below. "Wow," he says. "Weird. What does that feel like from the inside?"

I laugh. "Even weirder. What's bugging you, Reid? Part of you isn't really here."

He takes his hand away and goes back to his place on the floor. "The Donkey wants to take me to Disney World . . . with the Donkeyette!"

The Donkey is the woman his father is currently dating. The Donkeyette is her daughter. "So go," I say. "You'll have fun. It's nice of her to ask."

He seems to pull his neck in, like a turtle. "She's trying to act like we're a family."

"Someday you probably will be. Your dad's got all the signs. The Donkeyette will be your sister. Like the Brady Bunch, Reid. You know?" I grab my hair and twist it up on top of my head. "And I'll be Alice, the lovable spinster who knows what you're feeling."

"You don't know anything," he tells me.

"No, you don't. You've got a chance to be in a sitcom here, Reid. Quit watching them and live it. Your father's giving you a family."

He scowls. "When that happens, you'll be history, you know!"

I sigh. "I'm going to college anyway. Everything changes. Like, for example, I didn't used to have this baby in my stomach. You know?"

"I know."

We both watch the screen, where Wally and the Beaver are nursing a sick baby alligator, rubbing beauty cream on its dry skin, feeding it milk and brandy with an eyedropper.

Mike Sullivan drives me home. I don't have a car. I have a savings account instead. "Loved the potato chips," I tell him.

He looks over and laughs. "When Jenna was pregnant with Reid, she had the biggest appetite." He's still in love with Jenna, even though she's been dead a long time. Mike is my role model for being a single parent. "Is everything okay with the baby?"

"Uh-huh. I saw the doctor last week. I hear you're going to Disney World."

He frowns a little. "It's Tina's idea. She thinks she can force a lot of love down Reid's throat. Do you know what he calls her?"

I giggle. "Yeah."

He looks at me seriously. "How can I make all this work?"

That pisses me off. Did I forget and wear my priest's collar again? Don't I look like a knocked-up high school senior? I want to tell him to call a hotline, but instead I say, "Mike, if I can get this to work," I point to my daughter, "you should be able to make your thing work. Reid doesn't know it, but he really wants a mother. That's why he's addicted to me and June Cleaver, in that order."

He laughs. "Yeah, but he wants to pick the mother; that's the problem."

"He's getting too old for a sitter," I say. "Maybe if I wasn't around so much, you know, he'd bond with her."

"Oh, I don't know. He looks over anxiously. "You're the only one he really talks to."

We're at my house. "Well, you'll both have to let me go

soon," I say, patting him on the arm as I get out. "Because I have to stop being a teenager in exactly three months."

"You'll always come back for the potato chips!" he calls after me.

It's a relief to hear him drive away. I want to be alone more than anything. But with a baby, you never really are. I trudge into the house, where my mother is watching *Who Wants to Be a Millionaire?*

"Sophie?" she calls when I'm almost in the clear.

I stop and lean on the wall.

She mutes the TV. "Sophie, can you just tell me one thing? No one . . . no one hurt you, did they? To get you pregnant? No one took advantage of you . . . ."

"No, Mom," I say quietly. "Nothing like that."

She sits back. "Thank you for telling me that."

I turn and almost stumble away. "Sure."

That night, in my dreams, I realize all the whales are female. They form a ring around me in the water and sing like violins.

3

Monday, when my alarm goes off, I know I'm not going to school. I'm the kind of person who can handle a lot of things, but then a certain mood comes over me and I just refuse to do anything. I guess if I wasn't like that, I'd never get any rest.

I put my arms over my head and give myself and the baby a good stretch, then snuggle in to enjoy the feel of being in bed: the clean, starched (and ironed, of course) sheets, my cotton nightgown, my own skin. I took a quiz in a magazine once about sensuality and found out I was a tactile person—my favorite sense was touch. That was the rarest, according to their chart. You have to shut off your brain to really feel things. That was probably the problem with all those non-tactile people. They didn't know how to shut off their brains.

Not a problem for me. I lie in bed for the next hour, listening to my mom get ready for work and finally go out the door. I guess she managed to suppress her anxiety that I'd miss school or that I might be bleeding to death or something. After she shuts the door, the house settles into a different state. Calmer. Happier.

I look out the window and watch the drift of a cloud and listen to a woodpecker drumming on the roof. Finally I get hungry and force myself out of bed.

It's only eight o'clock. I can still catch Joshua at home. I crawl up onto a stool in the kitchen, tucking my nightie around my legs like a fussy cat making a nest, and dial his number, bracing myself for the loud voice of his sister, Kimberly.

"Newport residence, this is Kimberly speaking."

"Hi, Kimberly." I poke through a fruit bowl and find an orange. "This is Sophie. Is Joshua still there?"

"Joshua is getting ready for school," Kimberly says. Joshua says when she grows up, she'll make a great prison guard or government informant. Her talents are self-righteousness and ratting people out, in that order.

"Can you get him for me?" I don't take any lip from ten-year-olds.

"Just a moment, please." I pull the phone away from my ear just before she drops it loudly against something.

While I peel my orange, I listen to a vague commotion in some distant part of Joshua's house. "And when I tell Mom, you'll get . . ."

"Go ahead!" Joshua says as he picks up the receiver. "Write up a damn report on me. I got a phone call. End of the world. Go type it up now, and I'll sign it, you little . . . Hey Sophie," he finally speaks into the receiver.

I dump my orange peels on the counter. "Tell her to put in her report that you're ditching school today."

"Uh . . . " Obviously Kimberly was hovering. "Yes, I think you're right, Sophie. I do have a test in American history today."

I take a big, juicy bite. "Make it up. It's a beautiful day. Look out the window."

"Yeah, it's the Revolutionary War. A fascinating period."

"It might be warm enough to go swimming. Or we could play Stop Now."

"I know. I worry about my grades, too. You know in order to stay on the team, I have to maintain . . . "

Kimberly's voice in the background. "This is total BS. What are you really talking about?"

"Why don't you get lost before I squish you like a bug?" Joshua says to her.

"You're supposed to drive me to school." Her voice is so smug, I can completely picture the face that goes with it.

"Oh, that's right. Sophie, I gotta go. I have to drive Kimberly to school."

I licked the juice off my fingers. "And then you can pick me up. I'll be ready."

There was a smile in his voice. "You got it."

Joshua inherited his old Buick convertible from his father, who had kept it in the garage for years, planning to restore it. This morning it makes a noise like safety pins shaking around in a jar as he pulls into my driveway. When he tries to put the top down, it sticks, and he has to stand on the backseat and shove it into place.

"Piece of junk," he mutters, as he slides back into the driver's seat. But he says it like a lover.

"Are you hungry?" I ask two blocks from home.

He sighs. "No, but you are. Right?"

I feign meekness. "All I had was an orange."

He shakes his head to show he thinks I'm hopeless. "It can't be a girl in there," he says, tapping my stomach. "It's got to be a whole soccer team."

"Don't call my daughter 'it.' Let's stop at Publix and get a picnic."

"Whatever. When you gonna name her? I thought that was imminent."

"Soon. She's trying to tell me in my dreams, but I can't remember."

He taps the baby again. "Speak up, honey. Tell Mama your name. Oh!" He raises his eyebrows. "Did you hear that, Sophie?"

I laugh. "No."

"She says her name is Joshuina!"

I pull down my sunglasses to give him a look. "I don't think so."

He shrugs. "It was worth a try." He pulls into a 7-Eleven. After sweeping the parking lot for anyone from school, we go in. I buy a loaf of starchy white bread, a pound of butter, a can of spray cheese, and a cinnamon roll. Joshua buys a two-liter bottle of Coke, a basketball magazine, and three lottery tickets. "I'm feeling lucky," he explains.

Something is definitely up with him, I think as we hit I-95. Nearing the ramp, he wets his finger, sticks it up in the air, and chooses south. We both get high from riding in the convertible. I'm a wind junkie and so is he. We know without saying that we're going to play our driving game, Stop Now. We pick a highway and direction and just roll. At some point somebody suddenly yells, "Stop now," and we take the next exit and explore whatever we find. We've made fabulous discoveries this way: a bunch of outdoor cafes in Delray Beach, a petting zoo in Deerfield, a Spanish monastery in North Miami. Other times all we find is a bad neighborhood. But that's a kind of adventure, too.

Joshua is happier than usual today. He's humming to himself and playing the drums by slapping his hands on the wheel. You can read Joshua's mind because he sings whatever he's thinking. I listen carefully to his humming over the rush of wind. Finally I make it out: "What Would Happen If We Kissed?" That's interesting, I think. "Did you call Acacia over the weekend?" I ask.

He slides his eyes over. "Stop that, witch!" he says.

"Don't use your powers on me."

"Not magic. I could tell from your singing."

"Oh." His fingers tighten on the wheel. He hates being such an open book, but what can I say? He is.

"Did you call her? Did you ask her out?"

"I'm blocking you!" he says. "I block your evil rays!" He starts purposefully humming "I Like Bread and Butter," both to block me and to mock my food choices.

"Eventually you're going to tell me about it," I say.

He grins. "Eventually. But not now."

I start humming "My Baby's Got a Secret." He joins in. I lean back and let the wind lift me all the way to the sky.

At the Julia Tuttle causeway exit, my baby starts kicking the heck out of me. I take that for a sign. "Stop now!" I shout, and Joshua immediately puts on the turn signal. It's easy from here to figure where we're going to go. Right before the causeway there's a little park that looks out over Biscayne Bay. There's nothing there, really, some gravel to park on, a little grass, a couple of benches; but we can both see it's perfect for a water-front picnic. No one is there except an old man fishing and about a hundred grackles who are strolling around, flipping gravel and poking in the grass for bugs. We park and carry our food to a stone bench, as far as possible from the old man, to give him and us privacy.

We don't talk. I shift from my wind spell to my water spell, mesmerized by the sparkle of the bay, where the waves come in layers, moving against one another like transparent silk scarves. Once in a while a boat goes by and the wake rolls in and splashes the rocks near our feet. I wonder if I'm really as happy as I think or if it's just hormones? I can't remember ever feeling so . . . in place.

"Okay, so I called her," Joshua says, pretending to watch the bridge go up.

I pretend along with him. This is the only way to get men to open up; you have to act like you're not especially listening. "And?"

"Well . . . we talked for a long time about you."

"And?"

He glances at me, then back to the bridge. "You know. She wanted me to say you weren't my girlfriend and that I didn't want you for a girlfriend and that you've never been my girlfriend and that if you ever did want to be my girlfriend, I wouldn't let you be my girlfriend. . . ."

"And what did you say to all that?"

"I said the truth. You're my best friend and you'll always be my best friend and I told Acacia I want her to be my girlfriend. And after I repeated all that about a hundred times, she said she'd go out with me this Friday."

"Good work!" I say. "And when she gets to know me, she'll know I'm not a threat. Let's eat." All I can think of is that soft, scrunchy bread.

Joshua twists the cap off the Coke bottle and uses it to scratch off his first lottery ticket. "Damn! Let's let the girl get to know me first." He grins. "Which I hope will happen on Friday night."

I laugh, unwrap the bread, and realize I have no knife for the butter. I scrounge in my purse for a tool, my stomach now screaming like a ravenous tiger. I can tell the difference between my hunger and my baby's hunger. She makes me scarf down food like a refugee. Before I was pregnant, I used to pick at my food and take hours to finish a meal.

The only thing I can find is my laminated library card. I gouge it into the heat-softened butter.

"Oh, gross!" Joshua says. "Damn!" he adds as he scratches his second ticket.

I don't care. I slather butter on the bread and top it with a layer of spray cheese. Then I put another piece of bread on top and squish it together. I gobble down the sandwich and then make another, taking more time with the second one.

Joshua finishes his last ticket. "Damn!" He stalks over to the trash can.

I wait till halfway through my second sandwich to ask the question I've been holding all weekend. His news about Acacia has slowed me down, but I know I still have to ask.

"I'm thinking of doing a Lamaze class," I tell him.

"Good for you." He swigs his Coke.

"Do you even know what that is?"

"Yes! I watch TV. They teach you how to breathe in labor. You go with your coach and . . . oh, no, Sophie. Oh, no. I don't like the way you're looking at me at all. Oh, no."

"Just listen to me for a minute," I say. "I just want you to listen."

"I'm listening," he says. "But as soon as I'm done listening, the answer is no!"

"I can't have my mother there."

"Sophie . . ."

"She'll upset me. She'll say all the wrong things and I'll get upset and this is scary enough without that going on."

"Sophie . . ."

"And I don't want to be alone. You know? I don't want to be alone, Joshua."

"You won't be alone. You'll have doctors and nurses and monitors."

"You know what I mean. Come on. You're my friend, and I need a friend."

"Sophie, look. Point one, you'll be naked. Point two, a kid is going to come out of you. Point three—you can't ask me to do like a girlfriend for you. I'm a guy. Point . . ." He's lost count.

"Four," I say.

"Point four, I know you have your troubles with your mother, but she's your mother. Not me. This is a time for her, not me. You need a woman and your real family. . . . "

"I need someone I can trust. I need someone I know can help me through this. You're that person, Joshua."

"And I tell you I'm not that person!" The fisherman glances around. Joshua lowers his voice. "There's things a man can do and things he can't and . . . "

I fold my arms. "This is because of Acacia." I know I'm making it hard for him, but I don't care. I'm desperate.

"Well, some of it is!" He sets down the Coke so hard, foam rushes out of the neck. "I spent three hours on the phone with that girl, convincing her you're not a threat, and the next minute you want me to gown up and catch your baby!"

"All you have to do is hold my hand. You don't even have to look where . . . "

"I'm not gonna look at anything! Because I'm not gonna be there. I'm not a hospital kind of friend, Sophie. I'm a telephone friend. I'm a hanging-out friend. . ."

"You're afraid Acacia will think you're the father if you're in the delivery room."

"No! I'm afraid of the delivery room itself! I'm afraid of the delivery!" He tries to joke with me, runs his voice up to falsetto. "I don't know nothin' about birthin' no babies!"

I can't help laughing, and then I realize I've been overlooking something, which I rarely do when I'm dealing with people. "This is about your father, isn't it, Joshua?"

His father's been dead less than a year. He was in the hospital in a coma for weeks after the car accident, before he finally died. "Are you scared to go back into a hospital?"

"No!" he cries. "No!" His voice cracks. He looks down. A tear spills out. "No."

I touch his arm." I didn't think of that. I'm sorry. I'm so wrapped up in myself now. . . "

He keeps his head down, still fighting off tears. "I'd put

bad luck on your baby, Sophie. If I was there, I'd just be thinking, Death, death, death. You don't want me there."

"I'm going to drop it now, Joshua, because I won't push you into something that will hurt you that bad. But just think. Maybe if you did it and saw a new baby happen, it could turn around how you feel about hospitals. Like break the spell."

He takes a breath so deep it shakes his big frame. "I don't know. We'll see," he says.

I know him. That's yes. "Thank you." I pull him into an awkward hug.

He pushes me off. "Make me one of those damn sandwiches!"

We get lazy and hazy in the afternoon sun. I eat my cinnamon roll, and we polish off the Coke like two old drunks, passing the bottle back and forth. Then he opens his basketball magazine. Maybe he's a little worn out from the joys of our friendship. I gaze at the water, letting it hypnotize me.

The sun burns pleasantly into my face. My baby is resting contentedly now, under my full stomach. Every few minutes the breeze kicks up, blowing a long, brown curl into my face and then back out again.

I become aware of the smallest sounds. The grackles in the trees, making a sound like rusty hinges. Joshua turning a page. The hiss and whiz of the old man casting his line. The lap of water on rock. The rising, falling tide of the wind.

I realize it's been a long time since a boat came by. The bay is so quiet. It seems as if the bridge hasn't opened in a long time. I look in that direction. I stare, breathing slowly, a little afraid to move. The Julia Tuttle causeway is gone.

I blink, because sometimes a little glitch in reality can be cleared up that way; but when I open my eyes, there is no bridge. There are no bridges at all. There is no highway behind me, no cars, no high-rises. I can't see the peninsula anymore. Just the big, unbroken round line of the bay. I'm not sitting on a bench. I'm sitting on the ground. On sand. Behind me the beach rises to a collection of high dunes. Beyond that I can see the tops of trees. Joshua is gone. The old man is gone.

Okay, I tell myself, I'm dreaming. I fell asleep in the sun, and I'm dreaming. But it feels as if I'm too alert, too awake. But maybe it always feels like that when you're in the dream, and you just don't remember. Vivid dreams in the third trimester, I remind myself. Just enjoy the fact that you're dreaming this beautiful landscape and go with it.

I look out to the bay now and see whales jumping in the surf, less than a mile offshore, within swimming distance. I find myself walking out to the surf, walking to the whales, greeting them. I feel as if I'm not pregnant anymore. I feel strong and athletic. I think I might be a man.

Now I stand in the surf, waist high, chanting something in a language I don't understand. But I know I am singing a hymn to the whales, asking them to help me, asking if one of them will lay down its life for me.

I begin to swim. I am a whale. The whales have shaped me into a whale as their answer to my song. They use their songs now to guide me to them. I understand all this, and it makes perfect sense. I feel joyful the whales have accepted my request.

Then I am a man again, riding on the back of a whale, like a cowboy in a rodeo. I know how to move and hold on as the whale jumps and bucks and beats her fluke against the water. It's hard to hold on, but I must hold on. Once the whale is chosen, it is a sin to let her go. Her life is a gift now, and it's a sin to refuse any gift. I raise my arm and see I am holding a spear.

I want out of this dream! The spell is broken, and I scream and scream to wake myself up! My scream shatters the water, and I am back on land.

Joshua holds me by the shoulders. "Hold still! Hold still! You'll hurt the baby!"

I look around me, hot, dazed, nauseated. Miami is back. I'm falling halfway off the stone bench; my leg is bruised. The old man is running over to us.

"It's okay!" Joshua calls to him. "She's pregnant. She had a bad dream. I didn't want her to flop around and hurt herself." He is saying all this in a rapid, nervous way because the old man looks suspicious of us as he approaches. Maybe he thinks Joshua was hurting me. Maybe he thinks we're on drugs. A lot of older people think all kids are on drugs.

"She's been having terrible dreams," Joshua keeps on explaining. He's sweating. He looks at me. "You okay now?"

"Yes," I say, and nod vigorously at the old man, who glares at us. "I'm fine now."

The old man says a curse word and walks away.

Free to be myself, I collapse against Joshua and cry.

"That bad?" he asks me. "Was it about those guys who chased you?"

I can sit up now. I wipe my face on my T-shirt. "No, no. Listen, Joshua, what were you doing when I was sleeping? Were you reading? Could you see me here?"

He blinks twice at the question. "I was reading. I didn't look up until you screamed. What are you asking? You think you were sleepwalking or something?"

I hug myself as a shiver runs through me. "No, I just don't think I had an ordinary dream."

"What do you think it was?" he asks.

I stare at the bay, the bridge, the high-rises, the boats and cars. "I don't have a word for it," I say.

I really can get by okay in classes; it's during the unstruc-
tured social times, like tonight, that the cone of silence
descends on me and isolates me. Joshua and I have analyzed it
to death. He thinks it's something I'm doing wrong, I think it's
something the other kids do to me. Maybe it's both. It started
in middle school when I had excuses to be unpopular; I was
fat, had acne, and my curly hair was a big, frizzy mess because
it hurt too much to run a comb through it. Also, I had a great
vocabulary, which is a bigger problem than you think. Like,
for example, one day in the fifth grade, this sixth-grade girl
who hardly knew me said, "Do you think you're cool?" My
clever response was, "I refuse to answer on the grounds it
might tend to incriminate me." Needless to say, she and her
friends devoted the whole year to chasing me down, attacking
me, and trying to get me to say other weird things like that. In
short, I was a freak in those days.

But now, to be perfectly frank, I know I've got a great
body (or at least I do when I'm not pregnant). My skin cleared
up, and when my hair is long, the weight keeps it from flying
in all directions. Except for English class, I no longer flaunt
my intelligence. I know I'm too blunt, and I look for argu-

ments; but I'm a pretty nice person on my good days, nicer than any of the cheerleaders, who run in a huge pack of loyal friends.

One way I would explain it is my mother's sister, my Aunt Tina. She got bitten by a rottweiler when she was four, and now, if she goes within a hundred yards of any dog, it starts snarling and jumping to get at her. She approaches dogs with shifty eyes and shaking hands, and they pick up on it. But she says she can't help it, and I totally understand what she means.

But Joshua thinks everything can be solved with a program of self-improvement. He's an athlete, so if he feels tired, he adjusts his carbs. If he misses too many free throws, he takes an extra hour of practice. So he thinks if I took a crash course in smiling and being friendly, I'd be prom queen in no time. It was on his advice that I went to my one and only school dance, last fall. The result of that little experiment is now growing in my abdomen.

Often Joshua will turn his back on his natural peer group, the male jocks and their gorgeous girlfriends, to be with me; but tonight he can't. We're dedicating the new gym in honor of Nestor Chanate, and Joshua was his best friend and teammate.

Eventually there will be a program, but right now we're having a "reception" with punch and cookies, which is pretty much like Dante's purgatory. I almost wish my mother would have come, because at least she would have clung to me and kept me from being alone.

All the jocks and coaches and female jocks and cheerleaders are dominating a huge space in the gym foyer in front of an upsetting blow-up poster of Nestor's face. There's also a gold plaque over the new gym door with Nestor's name and two dates, like a grave marker. The doors are closed, so later we can get the full impact of the gym. But sealed off like this, it feels like a big tomb, with Nestor's ghost waiting behind the doors to pop out at us.

Over his shoulder Joshua keeps throwing me nervous looks, which Acacia, who is holding his hand, always notices and follows up with a big frown in my direction. Once Joshua even motions for me to come over, but I shake my head violently.

Nestor's former girlfriend, Blanca Flores, is in the center of the group, sobbing and using up hundreds of borrowed tissues. Whenever her crying winds down, she looks up at the poster of Nestor to refresh herself. Nestor's face is beautiful in the poster. All eyes with long lashes and a weird kind of intensity . . . no, steadiness. Right now he looks more alive than anyone in the room. I see Mr. Kissanis coming toward me. Just what I need. I wedge myself farther into the corner, where I'm pressed like a cockroach and hold my punch cup up like a mask; but he comes anyway. He is holding one of his many children on his shoulder. I know from the shrieks in the crowd that several of his other children are here, too.

"Hi, Sophie." He shifts the toddler to his other shoulder. "I've been wanting to talk to you."

Heads turn in our direction. I wonder if Mr. Kissanis is on the short list in the betting pool of who the father is. If he wasn't before, he will be now. And the evidence of his virility is running all over the room.

"Oh yeah?" I look past him as if I'm dying to join a group of friends. He doesn't pick up on it.

"I'm so sorry for what I did to you in class a few weeks ago. I mean about reading your poem aloud. It was a terrible mistake. You know, teachers can make mistakes, too." He chuckles. The toddler on his shoulder waves its arms like a castaway signaling a ship.

"You meant well," I say listlessly. "You thought you were doing me a favor. You read the poem because you thought it was good."

"It was good. You're a very talented writer, Sophie. I want you to know that."

"I do know it," I say. Because I do not lie.

"It's so important that you give that talent a chance, complete your education."

"I'm enrolled at BCC in the fall."

"I know you are . . . but . . . it's easy to make plans now, but when the baby is a reality . . . I just hope you can keep from getting sidetracked."

As if on cue, Mrs. Kissanis appears at his side, one child holding each of her hands. A third, a little boy, runs up to Mr. Kissanis and throws his arms around his leg.

"Here you are!" Mrs. Kissanis is speaking to her husband, but she glowers at me. "I was looking everywhere for you. You have to go to the bathroom and talk to Philip. He's crying." Her voice and posture radiate exhaustion in direct proportion to her overly energized kids. I understand completely what Mr. Kissanis was telling me. If you aren't careful, children will steal your soul.

"Why is he crying?" Mr. Kissanis bounces his toddler hard.

"The poster, the dead boy, the whole thing." She gestures around at the room. "It just got to him."

"Daddy?" the leg hugger starts knocking on Mr. Kissanis's thigh as if it was a door. "Daddy?"

"He's too old for that!" Mr. Kissanis says. To the one on his leg he says, "Stop it!"

Mrs. K is losing her temper. "Well, no one told him he was too old for it. Will you please go talk to him?"

The little boy tries to knock again and hits his dad in the wrong place. "Oh!" Mr. Kissanis doubles over and has to juggle the toddler to keep from dropping it. When he straightens up again, he's mad at everyone. "Why don't you go talk to him?" he bellows at his wife. "If you're so sympathetic . . . "

She smirks. "He's in the boys' bathroom, Andrew." She says "Andrew" like you might say "stupid."

"DADDY!" screams the leg kid.

"What!"

"I have to go to the bathroom!"

Mrs. Kissanis grins. "There you go, Andrew. It's destiny."

Mr. Kissanis closes his eyes like he wants to yell. "Excuse me, Sophie." He hands the baby to his wife and takes off, trailing the leg-knocker, who is now holding the front of his shorts.

Mrs. Kissanis gives me her smirky smile. "Nice to have met you," she says as she walks away.

That's when I see her. Mrs. Chanate. Nestor's mother. I remember her from the funeral. Short, plump, raven black hair parted in the middle and drawn to a loose knot at the back of her neck. She looks like Nestor, has his high cheekbones and those calm, steady eyes. She stands in the doorway, gazing at the roomful of people. No one speaks to her. The hum of conversation drops a few decibels. She is more disturbing than the poster.

Ms. Rowling, the principal, walks over and puts an arm around Mrs. Chanate's shoulders, speaking very rapidly. Mrs. Chanate nods but does not make conversation. Ms. Rowling gestures frantically at things: the punch and cookie table, the poster, the door to the new gym. Mrs. Chanate nods but looks at other things: Nestor's group of friends, especially Blanca, who is staring back. Then she walks out from under Ms. Rowling's arm and serves herself some punch, still casting a bold, almost judgmental gaze around the room.

I think to myself, this could be my role model. She's a loner and doesn't feel bad about it—accepts it with pride. Something makes me walk over to her.

"Hello, Mrs. Chanate," I say, dipping punch beside her. "I'm Sophie Cooper. We met at your son's funeral."

She is still gazing out at the room. "Yes," she says. Her Spanish accent is heavy. "I remember you." She glances at me, then away. "When is your baby due?"

I'm a little startled. I know I stick out now, but I'm not used to it yet. "June. The first of June." And just like that, I know that's the baby's name. June.

"Are you afraid?" she asks me.

At first I can't even answer. No one has asked me that. Lots of other questions, but not that. "Sometimes," I say. Because I do not lie.

She scans me up and down. "You look very strong. You should do well."

I'm not sure if she means in labor or with the rest of my life. "Thank you," I say. I feel funny that we're talking about me at a time like this.

"Nestor was a nice boy," I say. "Everyone liked him."

Her eyes go inward. "I still look for him everywhere."

I'm trying to think of the right reply to that when Blanca comes running over and throws herself into Mrs. Chanate's arms, weeping and speaking Spanish too fast for me to follow. The only thing I make out is that she calls Mrs. Chanate "Mama."

Mrs. Chanate makes no move to push Blanca off. She just stands there like a brave person taking an injection.

I walk away from them.

My abdomen now extends 3.2 inches, or 8 centimeters, beyond my belly button. I've gained 19 pounds since last November. My baby, my daughter, June, weighs about 2 1/2 pounds. Dr. Mendez says that June's brain is adding tissue and developing ridges and indentations. I wonder if she's starting to be aware.

"You're doing absolutely great." Dr. Mendez fiddles with her earring as she gazes at my chart. "You were born to make babies, Sophie."

I laugh but don't want to leave that statement out in the universe. "I was born to write poems," I tell her. "Having this baby is a detour."

She looks up, very serious. "I hope you understand what a tremendous responsibility this is, Sophie."

I keep forgetting I look like a kid to everyone. That means I can't be honest. I have to only say BS things, so people won't think I'm going to sling Junie into a dumpster the minute she's born. "Oh, I know," I say, bowing my head like a nun. "I'm starting Lamaze tomorrow night."

"Oh, good!" she says. Then, carefully, "You're going with your mother?"

I take a deep breath. Dr. Mendez likes my mother, works with my mother. "No, with a friend. I . . . I don't want Mom to be in the delivery room."

She actually clucks her tongue. I've read about that but have never actually seen someone do it. "She's a nurse, Sophie. She's your mother. You can't tell me she doesn't want to be there."

"She does, but she gets me so upset. The one brochure you gave me said I had the absolute right to decide who should be with me in labor and who shouldn't."

She pulls up a stool. "How can you be uncomfortable with your own mother?"

"I don't know," I say. "But I am."

"Think how she will feel. She'll be working right there in the hospital. To be shut out . . . "

"What about how I feel? Are you worried about her being embarrassed or something? Is that the most important thing?"

Dr. Mendez pats her smooth, perfect hair. I've always dreamed of hair like that. Hair that would have weight and swing around your shoulders instead of flying in the breeze. "No, Sophie, the most important thing is your safe delivery. If you really feel you can't control your emotions around your mother . . . "

She's scolding me. I feel bad. Up until now, I've heard nothing but praise from her about my low blood pressure and my adequate pelvis. "I'm thinking of the baby!" I tell her. "That's who I'm putting first on that day!"

She nods, taps my chart with her pen. I see in her eyes she's not done. "You picked a girlfriend to be your labor coach?"

"No, he's a boy."

She hesitates. "The baby's father?"

I shake my head. "You know I want to keep that a secret."

We eye each other. She wants to go on, but I stare her down. She drops her eyes to the chart, flips to a different page. "Speaking of secrets, Sophie. You need to ask your mother again for something, anything about your father. Your baby needs to know as much as possible about her genetic history."

"I've tried," I say. "She clams up."

Dr. Mendez smiles. "Do you realize that makes you alike?"

I smile a little, too. I hadn't thought of it. "Maybe that's why we don't get along. But I'm not going to be like her. When June is growing up, I'll tell her about her father. I just . . . this is just what I want to do right now. It won't always be a secret. I think it's mean of my mother to keep me from knowing anything about my father."

"She's probably trying to protect you from something. But still, I want you to ask her again. We don't need the address and phone number. I just wish we could put down some facts about his medical history, if she knows them."

"I'll try."

"Okay." She pats my knee. "You can get dressed now."

"No, wait, Doctor. I want to ask you something."

She has started to get up, but she sits right back down.

That's what makes her a good doctor. She gives me her full attention, which actually makes it harder for me to speak.

"I've read all the books you recommended, and I can certainly see how pregnant women have a lot of weird symptoms. . . . "

She laughs. "Yes. What weird symptoms are you having?"

"Do pregnant women ever have . . . hallucinations?"

She tries not to react, but something flexes around the pupils in her eyes. She picks up my chart and begins flipping. "You had some spotting a month ago, right? Did I write a prescription for that? I don't have a note about it."

"No. You said to avoid exercise, and it just stopped by itself."

She frowns. "Oh. Tell me what you mean by hallucinations."

I tell her what happened in the park with Joshua. She bites her lower lip, getting ruby lipstick on her perfect white teeth. "That sounds more like a dream," she says.

"But I don't remember falling asleep. I felt like one minute the landscape was normal and the next, it had changed."

"But dreams are so deceptive, Sophie. Pregnant women get very tired. You could have fallen asleep fast and just not understood the transition. That's the only explanation that makes sense. And you've been under a lot of stress."

"No, I haven't."

"And you make it worse when you deny it. Didn't you tell me before you were dreaming about whales?"

"Yes, I dream about them all the time, but this . . ."

"Your baby . . . it's a good analogy . . . suspended in fluid."

"And I'm going to kill her with a spear?"

"Sophie, every pregnant woman has ambivalent feelings. That's what dreams are for, an outlet for forbidden wishes and concealed desires . . . "

I know in my bones this isn't true. "I don't think it was a dream."

Another stare down. "Is this the only . . . event . . . like this you've had?"

"Yes."

"If it happens again, call me immediately. Otherwise, just look at it like a dream that was very, very real. You know, you're a writer. Your imagination is stronger than most people's. And the textbooks are full of women having violent dreams in the last trimester. You have all your fears about the delivery . . ."

"Okay!" I say, to cut her off. I feel as if I'm back in Debbie Treadmore's office again.

"But if you do have any more episodes that trouble you, tell me right away. Weird chemicals are coursing around in you, and if something is out of balance, we need to know."

"Okay," I say. "Got it."

She makes a note in the chart and flips it shut before I can read it.

The next day there's a note shoved in the grate of my locker. I unfold it and I jump, because it's made from cut-and-pasted magazine letters. Something about the bright colors and the uneven sizes of the letters makes it seem extra crazy before I even read it.

YOUR A SLUT AND I WILL GET YOU. AND YOUR BABY TO.

I just keep reading it over and over, hoping it will change into something else. Hoping this is one of those vivid dreams. Hoping the whales will come along right now and take me far out to sea, where June and I will be safe from this crazy, illiterate person.

I wonder if I will tell anyone, even Joshua, about this. I

feel as if I want to hide it, like it's something bad I've done. I want to throw it in the nearest trash can, but I make myself study it for clues. It's a sheet of torn-out notebook paper. Some of the letters are pastel and swoopy, more like from a women's magazine than a men's. I peel one back and notice a funny smell. I sniff the paper. Nail polish. The person used clear nail polish as an adhesive. So I'm sure it's a woman, but I would have guessed that anyway. I think about my Lamaze class tonight and wonder if it's Acacia. She can't be happy Joshua is doing this with me. I don't know her very well, don't know if she could be this mean. But then, all the girls I've ever known since kindergarten have seemed mean to me. There isn't a girl in this school who really likes me, and it's gotten worse since Junie came along.

Instead of throwing the note away, I fold it over and over, until it's a tiny little packet; and then I tuck it in my bra for safekeeping.

As I start to walk on shaky legs, scanning every girl in the hall for French manicures, I feel June kicking me hard. She doesn't want that thing anywhere near her.

5

I should have known something was up when Joshua asked if he could meet me at the library, where they have the Lamaze class. He knows I don't drive and hates to see me taking the bus. Taking the bus is some kind of symbol for him that life is beating you down. It's just transportation to me.

If you take buses to places, you have two choices. You can arrive fashionably late or geeky early. I choose geeky early, and there are no signs (literally) of a Lamaze class anywhere in the library. Like a fool, I go to the information desk for information. A woman with Coke bottle glasses hollers over her shoulder to a woman with a bald spot. "Is there some class tonight?" It doesn't matter that she yells. Except for the three of us, the library is deserted.

"I don't think it's tonight," the other one says. She's eating a sandwich behind the desk. I feel as if civilization is breaking down before my eyes.

"Yes, it is," I say in my helpful Girl Scout voice. I dig in my purse for the paper they mailed me and accidentally come up with my hate letter that I brought to maybe show Joshua. At the sight of it, adrenaline floods me, and I miss several seconds of what's going on in front of me.

When I can function again, they've produced a third woman from somewhere. She's about six-foot-seven and holds a ring of keys. "It's not until seven-thirty!" she scolds me.

I hope to God this is not the instructor. I look at my watch and see it's twenty after seven.

"I'll let you in," she growls. "But don't move any chairs!"

I follow her, suppressing hundreds of sarcastic replies. She leads me down a side hall past bathrooms. I take note. These days I always like to know where the bathrooms are. She unlocks the door and knocks down a kind of kickstand to prop it open.

The light in this room is so fluorescent, it feels as if I'm underwater. A piano, painted the color of banana pudding, sits against one wall. Tables and chairs are pushed against one another. We're probably going to sit on the floor, I think, struggling to work myself into one of the chairs without moving it. The mailer told me to bring a pillow, but I wasn't going to lug that on the bus.

I don't like the room. It's cold, and the overhead lights hum like bees. There are huge, construction paper dinosaurs on the wall, leftovers from storytime, no doubt. I feel big and small at the same time.

A couple comes in, straight from a sitcom about a happy, happy marriage. I start up a lecture in my head about not letting this bother me while the sitcom lady, who clearly loves everyone, comes over and sticks out her hand. Under the lights, her shiny hair almost blinds me. "Hi, I'm Kathy." She rests her free hand on her abdomen, which is gigantic compared to mine. "Is your husband parking the car?"

Just jump right in, says the lecturer in my head. "I'm not married," I say. "My name is Sophie Cooper."

To her credit, Kathy still beams at me. "Good for you!" she says. She points to her husband, who is still shedding backpacks, pillows, and supplies like a tall, skinny mule. "That's Dick."

"Hi, Dick," I say with a perfectly straight face.

Dick says hi.

Luckily Joshua walks through the door right then. And right behind him, looking gorgeous, is Acacia! She walks right up to me, puts her arms lightly around my neck, and says "Hi, Sophie" as if we're friends.

Joshua has his hands in his pockets, a sign he's uncomfortable. "Hey," he says, eyeing me warily to see if I'm going to pitch a fit at his little surprise. Dick and Kathy watch with interest. I try to think what this looks like. Maybe they think I'm one of those surrogate mothers like they've seen on *Inside Edition*.

It's seven-thirty now and the other couples are pouring in the door, giving me time to think. Acacia came because she likes Joshua and wants to get closer to his friends. Acacia came because she's jealous of me and is trying to get over it. Acacia came because she's jealous of me and wants to destroy me. Acacia came because Joshua is uncomfortable being here, and he begged her. Acacia came because she wrote the note and wants to see if she's driven me mad yet. It burns in my purse. I can't show it to Joshua now.

The instructor finally comes in at seven forty-five. I make a note to take the later bus next week. Her name is Charlotte Hemmings, and she's nothing like I pictured. I was thinking of a blonde in her twenties with a ponytail, like an aerobics instructor. Charlotte Hemmings is fortyish and bony with a bad orange perm and a patchwork dress.

She herds us onto the floor (Kathy loans me one of her pillows) and starts lecturing (Kathy loans me paper and a pen). I look around the room and see all the couples sitting the same way, the women in the protective V of their husband's legs, leaning back against them, encircled by loving arms. And I see my little threesome of awkward teenagers, all careful not to touch one another, as Charlotte Hemmings trills on about intimate body processes. Hormones flood me, tears of self-pity rise like a tidal wave. I am doing this all alone, I think. All alone.

June starts to throw a tantrum. It feels as if she's beating her fists and kicking her feet. I get the message. She wants me to remember this is not about me. This is about her. I put my attention back on Charlotte Hemmings and take notes.

After class Joshua insists we go to Baskin-Robbins. I can see he wants Acacia and me to get along. He doesn't know she might be threatening to kill me. I stare at them from the backseat of his car. She is beautiful: her hair a waterfall of tiny braids that must take hours to do, her makeup flawless, her nails an iridescent silver tonight. She probably goes to a salon to have these things done, I think. She wouldn't have a bottle of Sally Hansen sitting around the house at all.

"What a bunch of clowns!" she says of the class. Her perfect hand drapes along Joshua's arm. I feel a pang of something. "Let's get some ice cream, honey."

He mutters something about that sounding like a plan. I'm reeling from "honey." They just started going out! I want to ask them to drop me off at home, but June is begging for her favorite flavor, mandarin chocolate sherbet.

Acacia hooks her elbow over the seat back. "Honey," she says to me. "We need to go shopping, girl. You're way past the big T-shirt stage. You need maternity clothes. My sister told me, only two good things you get out of being pregnant. You can eat like a pig, and you have to buy new clothes."

"And you get a baby, too," I remind her. I'm relieved to find out that everybody is "honey."

She waves her pretty nails, dismissing the baby. "That's a long way off. I'm talking about now. Are you free on Saturday?"

Joshua's eyes flick to the rearview mirror. Oh, please, oh

please, be nice to my girlfriend, Sophie.

But he doesn't know she could be stalking me. "I have to be really careful about money," I say. "I'm saving for college."

"Then I know just where we should go." Her smile is dazzling, scary. I used to dream about having pretty, popular girls like her meeting me at malls and trying on shoes with me. Now I'm afraid. She's trying to corner me alone, away from Joshua, and then she'll move in for the kill.

Joshua's almost swerving off the road, he's glaring at me so hard. She's trying to be nice. What's your problem?

"Okay, great, Saturday it is." I'm tired, out of arguments.

At Baskin-Robbins Acacia teaches me you can get extra syrup and no whipped cream on your sundae just by asking for it. "And give her three cherries," she tells the kid. "She's pregnant."

She's going too far out of her way for me, like all the psychopaths I've ever seen in the movies. But Joshua looks so happy. And it is the best sundae I've ever had in my life.

My hands shake as I take the old picnic basket down from the kitchen shelf. It smells like ancient dust, like how old tree ornaments smell when you take them out of the box. It reminds me of how long it's been since Mom and I had fun.

Even as I walked up to the front door, I heard the stereo playing. Today is the day the teddy bears were having their picnic . . .

It had been a bad day at school. I was in the third grade. I'd screwed up a math problem at the board; somebody at lunch had made fun of my thermos bottle (Scottie dogs); and a bunch of boys chased me home, trying to pull up my dress, which was the "in" thing that week.

But I opened the door and there was Mom, who had worked an eight-hour nursing shift, but had changed into capris and a shirt printed like a red bandanna. She had spread a checkered cloth on the living-room floor. All the teddy bears she could find, big and small, were seated around the cloth in front of plates and cups. "Teddy Bears' Picnic" was set on repeat, the spooky, bouncy melody making my weary body want to dance.

The picnic was designed around what bears might like—peanut-butter-and-honey sandwiches, iced herbal tea, blueberries and cream. Within five minutes I had forgotten the whole rotten day, and I know she had done the same.

My picnic today isn't so well thought out. But I try to incorporate her favorite things. Cheddar cheese slices on dark rye bread. Nutter Butter cookies. A thermos (no Scotties this time) of iced coffee with milk and sugar. As a final thought, I slip in a teddy bear. Maybe she'll remember, and everything between us will be fixed. I know I have to try. If not for me, for June. I feel like if I can repair the damage between Mom and me, maybe June will never turn on me, and we can be friends forever. Plus, my mother has information June needs, and we're going to get it.

When I get to the nurses' station, she isn't there, but I know the nurse behind the desk. Jackie Simmons. Jackie is really nice. I wish she could be on the OB floor when Junie comes. She looks up when she hears the elevator open and shoves the pen she's using into her hair. "Oh, look at you, Sophie. That basket is bigger than you are! Here, let me help you."

She trots over and takes it for me. People have been doing things like that lately. I must really be getting huge. "Does your mom know you're here?"

"No," I say, blushing like a guy calling for his prom date. "It's a surprise."

"Oh! You sure picked the right day. She's in Mr. Murdock's room again. She might as well camp in there, the way he leans on the call button. He wants the bed up, he wants the bed down. . . hey, why aren't you in school?"

I practice my lie. "In-service day," I say.

"And you wanted to spend it with your mom. That's so sweet. Let me get her." She depresses the intercom. "Beth?"

My mom's voice sounds out of breath. "Now what?"

"Come down to the desk and see!" Jackie disconnects. "See? She's having a real hard day. This will be great."

I hope so.

My mother rounds the corner, flushed and furious, head down like the cow-catcher on a train. But when she sees me, she's derailed. "Oh!"

"It's a teachers' in-service day, and I thought it would be fun to surprise you with a picnic lunch," I babble wildly. "Remember? How we used to have picnics all the time when I was little?"

She looks wary. "Of course, I remember."

"Can you take your lunch break now?" My voice is high and squeaky.

She glances at Jackie. "Go!" Jackie says. "I'll cover for you."

Mom lowers her head again and walks past me to the elevator. "This is nice of you," she mutters.

I grab the basket and wobble-run to catch up.

We find a bench outside that isn't covered with smoking interns, and I spread everything out like a nervous maitre d'. She looks so astonished, I wonder how hostile I've been to her lately. For the first half hour, I let her complain about Mr. Murdock and the call button. Gradually she sits back and stops looking at her watch. She is twisting open a Nutter Butter when I say, "I had a really good checkup."

She flinches at the reminder I'm pregnant but dutifully says, "Your BP was good? What's your weight now? You're taking your vitamins, aren't you?"

I tell her my blood pressure was fine and answer all her questions, then say, very softly, "Dr. Mendez asked if I could get any information about my father."

She slaps the Nutter Butter down as if it were poison. "Oh. So all this was to soften me up."

"No." I'm surprised to find tears in my eyes. "It's because I'm going to have a daughter, and it makes me remember what a good relationship we used to have and I—I never want June to have a bad relationship with me."

"Who's June?"

"The baby."

"Where did you get that name?"

"From when she's due. Don't you like it?"

She blinks. "I guess I should just be glad she's not coming in February."

Eggshells seem to be everywhere all of a sudden. "Tell me if you don't like the name."

She shrugs. "It sounds like you already decided by yourself."

"But I'm trying to get you involved right now. I need to know about my father for medical reasons. Just give me a name, and I'll take it from there."

"You'll do what? You're talking about trying to track him down?"

Crunch, crunch. "He is my father," I say.

"Only technically."

"But . . ."

"If you could forget about him, half the problems we have would be solved."

I wonder what the other half is. "My doctor told me . . ."

"Don't give me that lame excuse. You want to know for yourself because you want to go find him. But there's nothing to find, Sophie. He's a guy who got me pregnant. He doesn't want to have anything to do with you, believe me."

"Are you ever in touch with him?"

"God, no."

"Do you know where he is now?"

"I wouldn't tell you if I did. Look, why should I tell you anything when you won't tell me who the father of my grand-child is? It's that Joshua, isn't it?"

"I don't want to play guessing games."

"Neither do I. Do you think you're protecting him?"

"It wouldn't be fair to this person to tell his name."

"Fair to him! He got you pregnant. How is he fair to you?"

"It's . . . he . . . "

"There. See? You can't have it both ways. But just so you'll leave me alone: I don't know where your father is, I don't know a thing about his medical history, and I wouldn't try to find him if I were you. There are worse things than not knowing who your father is. Trust me."

Something makes our eyes lock. I think of something that never occurred to me before. "Mom? Were you . . . "

"I'm late." She gets up and walks past me like a wind blowing.

It's a long, hot walk back to the house. I hold the heavy basket with both hands so it won't bump the baby. I think about all the people inside me: my mother, my baby, the stranger who is my father. Maybe he was a stranger to her, too. Maybe he was just a shadow in an alley behind a nursing school. Maybe she sees him every time she looks in my face . . . maybe half of me is criminal, or crazy. Maybe . . . I step off the curb. The bus is huge, honking, air brakes hissing as it skids, the grill rushing into my face. I'm going to die! But then something happens, and I'm plunging into water that shouldn't be there. Dive, dive, dive when danger approaches. Lie on the bottom, silent. Hold your breath. Our only enemy is man.

I must be dreaming, I think. Or this is a brain reaction to death, a soothing fantasy as my brain cells shut down. Because a minute ago I was in Fort Lauderdale and a bus was going to hit me, and now I'm a whale, lying still in the soft, warm, rocking, dark blue water. I'm holding my breath, but it's easy. Deep, rolling sounds fire off around me, and I know what they mean. A school of fish to my left, a reef behind me. I'm echolocating.

I have a feeling in my body like when you're dreaming and start to wake up. Good, I think, then I'll hear the ambulances, see my own blood showering the air; but at least it will be real.

I swim to the surface. At first I swim by rippling my fluke; but later I have arms, and I use them to pull at the water, because my lungs are starting to hurt. I claw at the water, break the surface, am blinded by the dazzling sun.

I'm back at Key Biscayne. I'm in the water at Biscayne Bay in Miami, miles from where my brain thinks I should be. I'm either insane or something magical has just happened.

With the last of my strength, I swim to shore, slosh up on the bank in my wet sundress and soaked tennis shoes. I don't know where my purse or the picnic basket are.

I crouch on the shore a long time, drying in the sun, waiting to see if I'll completely crack up. Finally I walk a few blocks and panhandle enough change to page Joshua, who calls me back twenty minutes later at the pay phone. He'll have to miss another test, but he agrees to come get me. I tell him I don't want to explain or even talk very much, so we ride back home in peace. He puts the classical station on the radio.

He goes back to school for sixth and seventh periods. I go home and lie in bed, just lie very still, afraid to think about anything.

Want to know what boring is? Boring is babysitting a thirteen-year-old boy who's on the computer in a wrestling chat room. That's boring.

"Reid!" I whine. "Shut that thing off. Play with me!"

He can't even hear. His face is washed in the aquarium light of the monitor. His eyes track the words of wisdom typed by his invisible friend, Stingmark.

> the intruder is lame.

Reid's name is Powerbomb 3:16. He answers.

> yeah, he's lame. what do you think of the homewreckers?

Stingmark answers:

> awesome. and their valet, brandi, is so cool.

Reid types enthusiastically:

> huge guns!

Okay, even I understand that!" I explode. "Log off now, Powerbomb, or I'm telling your dad!"

Reid swivels and looks at me with basset hound eyes.

"I'll tell him you're talking about breasts on the Internet! I swear I will!" I fold my arms on top of my stomach.

Reid turns back to the keyboard, muttering that I am a "real cranberry." Whether that is Internet slang, wrestling slang, or rap slang, I have no idea. Reid is fluent in all three.

GOTTA GO, he taps. THE REF IS CALLING FOR THE BELL.

WHEN DO YOU USUALLY LOG ON? Apparently Stingmark is hungry for more intellectual stimulation.

TOMORROW. 5:30, Reid promises.

GREAT. OH, AND DID YOU KNOW I'M A GIRL? BYE.

Reid stares at the screen. Then at me. "Look what you made me do!" he cries. "I was talking to a girl who likes wrestling." He runs his hand through his spiky blond hair. "What if I never find her again?"

"It would be a tragic love story," I say. "Right up there with Tristan and Isolde."

"Who?"

"They were a famous tag team from the Middle Ages."

He laughs, paws the popcorn I made earlier. "So what do you want to do?"

I suddenly have a brilliant idea. "You're pretty good with that computer, aren't you, Reid? Could you search out some information for me?" I don't know much about computers compared to everyone else. It was one more thing, like a car, that I decided I didn't need so I could save more money for college. I have gone to the library and practiced word processing, though. I want to be able to type my term papers this fall.

"You name it, I search it." He taps a series of keys and pulls up a box that says SEARCH FOR KEYWORD with a blank to fill in.

I hesitate. "Shape-shifting."

He swivels to look at me. "Huh?"

"I'm working on a poem," I say. Thank God for poetry. You

can bring up any wacky topic in the world and say it's for a poem.

He searches. They offer us several hundred choices. We scan and sample. I find out very quickly that there are some frightening people on the Internet, some of whom think they are real vampires. Nobody seems to be changing into a whale, though.

"This is creeping me out," Reid says, as he pulls up "The Dungeon of Merlin" and we read some gothic script about "The Beast."

"Yeah, this isn't what I want. Try whales."

"Whales!" he says. "Is this the same poem?"

"It's a series of poems."

He taps away. "About werewhales, I guess. Really nice."

There are even more sites for whales than for shape-shifters. Most of them are set up for kids, telling whale facts and statistics. I linger in several places. One tells about whale body language and what it means. I learn, for example, that beating the water with your fluke is an alarm call. I figure if I'm going to swim with them, I'd better learn their language.

At another site, we download and play whale sounds. They're beautiful, like babies' cries mixed with French horns, like the sounds I've heard in my dreams. Junie comes to life at the sounds and makes rhythmic movements, like she's swimming. I learn that whales evolved from canines, and that they are at the top of the oceanic food chain. *Our only enemy is man.* Then I see something good: WHALE MYTHS.

"Click on that!" I tell Reid. "Click on that."

It's not what I thought. It's stuff like, MYTH: A WHALE IS A FISH. FACT: IT'S A MAMMAL LIKE YOU AND ME. "I'm not going to find what I want." I stuff popcorn into my mouth. It tastes oily and stale.

"Tell me what you want," Reid says. "You're picking the wrong keywords."

I wonder if I could tell him. I know I'd rather confide in

a kid than in my obstetrician or my school counselor, both of whom would probably feel as if they had to put me in a mental institution. I don't want June to be born at the Sunny Breeze Center for Troubled Teens.

I look into Reid's big blue eyes and think how good it would be to tell someone. But then I think that's selfish. Bad enough to have a crush on your eighteen-year-old pregnant babysitter. He shouldn't have to be a mental health counselor, too.

"Try . . ." I struggle to think of a different angle. "Biscayne Bay."

He turns back to the monitor, shaking his head. "Must be a horror story. 'The WereWhales of Biscayne Bay.'"

"Do me a favor, Reid. Just for once in your life, try not to put two and two together."

Biscayne Bay has about thirty references we can look up. I see HISTORY under Biscayne National Park and have Reid click on that.

He clicks. We read about the arrival of the Spanish and about the Tequesta Indians who lived there before that and how they fished and hunted sea turtles and whales.

"Whales!" Reid says, as I shiver. "We have a match."

"Get out of there," I say. "And look up Tequesta."

Reid taps quickly, caught up in my excitement, even if he doesn't understand it. Under TEQUESTA we find a reference to the Miami Circle.

"Remember that?" Reid says. "Our class went down there to protest."

It's a prehistoric stone circle. They unearthed it when they were breaking ground for a hotel. The developers wanted to destroy it, but the whole community rallied to save it. I wonder now what part of the bay it's on.

"Click there." I point at the screen. TEQUESTA HISTORY AND CUSTOMS.

We find pictures of people wrapped in animal skins, throwing spears, living in thatched huts, making stone tools. We read about how they hunted whales by riding on their backs and spearing through the blowhole. My whole body gets very cold and still as I remember my dream. Whales were sacred to the Tequesta who lived in and around Biscayne Bay. The Tequesta worshipped the sun. The stone circle is thought to be a marker for the solstices. The Spanish destroyed the Tequesta, killed and completely drove them out. There are no Tequesta left in Florida.

"Cool," Reid says as we finish the page. He exits and turns to me. "What's all this got to do with you?"

I shake myself awake. "Like I said. I'm working on a poem."

He grins. "Must be a whale of a poem! Be sure and show it to me."

"Okay." I feel weird, as if I'm listening to two things at once. I'm glad I found a link between some of these things that have been haunting me. But Reid's question is a good one. What does a lost, forgotten tribe of Indians want with me?

The next morning I realize I have nothing to wear to go shopping with Acacia. Can you go shopping to get ready to go shopping? Nothing that I think would look good fits me anymore. I know that even without trying, she will look fantastic. But that's the purpose of the exercise, right? I'm supposed to learn from her. So I put on my jeans with the safety pin that I've been wearing every day this month. Now the safety pin hardly reaches across my abdomen. I cover the whole thing with a gigantic pink T-shirt printed with seashells that I had bought at Target. I realize now that this T-shirt was created and marketed just for tourists, but I bought it. Acacia has her work cut out for her. I complete my look with a pair of five-dollar Payless sandals and my worn-out brown vinyl purse. Since I look like crap anyway, I pull back my hair in a rubber band. It's been bothering me lately and I'm afraid if it bothers me too much, I'll cut it off.

I find my mom in the hall, enjoying her day off by cleaning out the linen closet.

"I'm going shopping," I say as I hurry by.

Of course she follows me. "Want me to go along?"

I avoid eye contact. "I'm going with a friend."

She folds her arms, brow creasing. She has permanent lines in her forehead from frowning at me. "Not with that Joshua!"

I sit on the couch, rebuckling my sandal. "No. His girl-friend, Acacia."

She walks around me, trying to get me to look up, but I refuse. "Acacia. I suppose she's black, too."

I look up now. To let her see the genuine horror and astonishment on my face.

She steps back. "Well, I'm sorry! Can't you have any white friends?"

Because there is a God, this conversation is interrupted by a car horn outside. I walk past my mother fast enough to make a breeze and mutter, "You can be my white friend, Mom."

As predicted, Acacia looks perfect, even though there is nothing special about her outfit. She has a pair of hemmed cutoffs that fit her perfectly and a ribbed yellow top with a slightly scooped neck. Her braids are tipped with bright yellow baubles. She wears a big tank watch and has a good leather purse and sandals. She starts the lesson immediately, fingering my seashell shirt.

"You should only wear this kind of thing to bed."

She doesn't say it mean, but I get defensive anyway. I glare at her as she starts the car. I wonder what it's like to have a car and not have to trudge to bus stops and wait in the hot sun.

"I'm saving up to go to college, you know!" I shout into the wind. "My mother can't afford to send me, and I'm determined to go!"

Her eyes slide over. "I can respect that."

I adjust my volume. "My point is, I don't have a lot of money to waste on just looking good; and I mean, I appreciate your help today, but I guess you need to know, I can't spend more than fifty dollars, and I shouldn't even spend that." I went to the teller machine last night and deposited several checks from Mike and for the first time since I started my account, made a withdrawal. Now it seems like a mistake. Fifty dollars was a lot of money in a bank account; but in a retail store, it wouldn't buy much more than a good pair of jeans.

Acacia takes a pair of sunglasses from the dashboard and slides them on. She looks like a TV star. "Could you go seventy-five in an emergency?"

My voice gets loud again. "What kind of emergency comes up when you're shopping?"

She swings her head to glance at me, baubles clacking. "Sophie. You have no clothes. You're getting bigger and bigger. I was looking to get you a whole wardrobe today, one that you can use now and for school in the fall. If you buy the right things, you can belt them in after the baby comes."

I fold my arms. "You want to buy me a whole wardrobe for fifty dollars?"

"Seventy-five," she corrects. She glances at my purse. "You need accessories, too."

"And just how do you plan to accomplish this miracle?" I ask.

She flashes her TV star smile. "It ain't what you do, it's the way you do it, Sophie. That's a song."

We start at a creepy little shopping center at the corner of

Oakland and US One. It's a shopping center I'd never go in, dominated by a piano and organ store and an electric razor repair shop.

Acacia throws the car into park. "You see, Sophie," she says, pulling her sunglasses down her nose and looking at me comically. "You can spend five dollars at Kmart getting an ugly giant T-shirt or—" she gets out of the car and I follow—"you can spend five bucks on something yummy that some rich woman just got tired of." She stops in front of a tiny storefront. The sign says What Goes Around.

"Secondhand!" I shout like a true convert.

"Watch and learn." Acacia pushes through the door, and a bell rings like in an old-time movie. An Indian woman in a beautiful gold sari is reading a battered paperback behind the counter. "Hello, Rajathi!" Acacia says. "We're going to fix up a little maternity wardrobe for my friend Sophie. And, of course, I might see something for myself."

The woman smiles without looking up from her book. It's *Stranger in a Strange Land*. I know how she feels.

The store is so full of stuff, my brain shuts down, and I can't see anything. Racks are crammed with clothes, marked off by size. Jewelry is piled in plastic bins on the counter. There is a cardboard box full of shoes on the floor. My hand reaches out to a rack of baby clothes.

Acacia props her sunglasses on her head and studies me. "The first surprise is that you don't look good in that color of pink. I always thought of you as light, but you have kind of an olive skin. I'm going to call you an autumn."

I have no idea what she's talking about. She takes one more look at me, clearly judging my stomach dimensions, and heads for a rack, sifting through it like a human threshing machine, pulling out what she wants and piling it on the counter. A denim jumper. An ivory-colored dress printed with tiny sunflowers. Four T-shirts and a green dress with a high waist.

"Get to work." She points to the dressing area. "I want to see each and every thing including how the color of each T-shirt looks with your skin. Meanwhile . . ." She digs into a pile of costume jewelry like a greedy pirate.

In the dressing room I look at all the tags, marked with ballpoint pen. The most expensive thing is the sunflower dress. Thirteen dollars. Just for a second I want to cry.

Acacia approves of the ivory, gold, and olive T-shirts but throws the maroon one back. The green dress is thumbs-down, but the sunflower dress, which I love, is thumbs-up. The jumper, she says, will be essential. Meanwhile, she runs up to me holding scarves and pieces of jewelry to my face. She adds an ivory chiffon scarf and a string of pearls to the pile, then as an afterthought, puts back the pearls and adds a gold locket. My heart flutters as the cash register chugs and rings like a slot machine. My total is thirty dollars.

Acacia picks out a purse for herself that looks like quilted black leather, and we're off. "Where to next, Fairy Godmother?" I ask. My voice is high and giddy.

She shifts into reverse. "Holy Cross Hospital."

"Huh?"

"Great thrift store. And clean bathrooms. I remember when my aunt was pregnant. I'm sure you have to go by now."

Maybe she really is my fairy godmother.

By three o'clock I have the most beautiful wardrobe I could imagine plus three little outfits for June. I spend a total of eighty dollars (there was a teller machine next to Holy Cross), but now I understand it's better to spend $80 with a plan than keep dribbling five dollars here and there on tourist T-shirts. I also find out the sky doesn't fall if you just eat a candy bar for lunch. Acacia suggests going to my house and "playing" with all my new purchases, but I picture my mother there, running the vacuum and noticing who's black and who's white, so I suggest we go to Acacia's house instead. She hesitates. She calls her house. No one picks up. Then it seems to be okay. Aren't there any parents anywhere who want their kids to have friends?

Of course, her house is much nicer than my condo, but I expected that. Her bedroom is all decorated with things that match, and she has one of those vanities where you can sit down and primp in front of a mirror. I don't know how to primp, but I sit there anyway, enchanted with my reflection in my new ivory tunic and rust-colored pants with a nice, comfortable, stretchy waist. I'd love to try on one of her lipsticks, but I'm afraid they'll be too dark for me.

She's sitting cross-legged on her bed, putting things from her old purse into her new purse, which she explains is Chanel-style. "You look great, Sophie," she says, her reflection talking to my reflection. "Now take that raggedy rubber band out of your hair, and I'll show you how to tie your hair back loosely, with the scarf."

I yank out the rubber band along with a lot of hair. "Where's your brush?" I ask.

She laughs like a little kid. "Honey, you're in a black girl's room. If I used a brush I'd look like a brush! You shouldn't use one either, or those rubber bands. That's why your hair is all breaking and frizzing like it is. I bet you blow it dry, too."

"Well, I have to," I say. "Or it comes out so curly I can't even get a comb through it."

She gets up, takes a spray bottle of something, and starts squirting my hair. "Oh, honey. Who raised you? You could be accused of hair abuse. From now on you wash it, you use a leave-in conditioner, and you let the air dry it. And you never, ever try to put a comb through it." She takes a wide-toothed pick and works it through my hair, very gently. "See? That will make it look neat, without ripping it out of your head. You try."

I think back to when I was four, my straight-haired mother dragging a brush through my hair while I cried. She didn't know. The stuff Acacia has sprayed on my hair has tamped down the frizz, and little curls are forming, like you see on the beautiful, curly haired women on TV.

"Then"—she takes the chiffon scarf, gathers my hair gently below the back of my neck, and ties it in. "You make a loose ponytail, never tight like you had it. Let the curls have room to breathe. See?"

Little tendrils curl around my cheeks like sweet pea vines. I shake my head, and it feels right. I have never felt so beautiful. "Acacia?" I say in almost a whisper.

She's looking at me like an artist looks at a well-done canvas. "What?"

"Why have you been so nice to me today?" I know I'm spoiling it, but I have to ask anyway.

She looks hurt. "We were having fun. Weren't we?"

"Yes, but . . . well, I mean, you have a lot of other friends. Why are you paying attention to me all of a sudden like this?"

She walks away and sits on the bed. I think to myself. You blew it.

"You come right out with things, don't you?" she asks me. "Joshua said you were like that. He likes that about you. Okay, if you have to put it like that . . . I just never noticed you much, Sophie. You're so quiet in school. It wasn't like I was snubbing you or anything. . . . "

"But now, because of Joshua, you've decided to be friends with me . . . so it wouldn't be so . . . weird . . . right?"

"Partly." She starts chewing on her thumb, catches herself, and stops. "I mean, I admit I . . . a lot of kids think it's odd . . . your friendship with him. People think . . . a lot of people think . . . "

"It's his baby."

"Yes. But I don't think that, because he told me you're

just friends, and I don't think he's a liar. So when he and I got together . . . I thought you and I should be friends so we could all be friends and . . . " She starts up the thumb chewing again.

"And what?"

"Because you're pregnant. I want to be your friend because you're pregnant . . . . I know . . . you must feel so different from everyone else, and the kids in school stare at you, and I don't think that just because you and some boy made a mistake you should be . . . isolated. This is a time when you need . . . " She breaks off, and I see she's crying.

"Acacia?"

"If I had had one good friend . . . " she says into her hands. She's hardly talking to me now, more to herself.

"What are you . . . "

"At my other school. Before I came here. My junior year."

My voice lowers. "You got pregnant, too?"

She starts crying loud and hard. " . . . yes."

"What happened? You lost the baby? You gave it up?"

Shaking her head, crying and crying. " . . . ortion. They made me have . . . "

"Okay," I say. "I get it." I go to her, carrying the tissue box. She pulls them out rapid-fire. Blows her nose. Clears her throat. "My mom and dad said it would ruin my future. My boyfriend turned on me, said he didn't think it was his when he knew it was. All my friends at that school, all my so-called friends, treated me like I had a disease. Suddenly people acted like I was trash. Even my . . . " She glances toward the bedroom door. "It was all this pressure to make it like it never was. And I wanted to get back to where people treated me well again . . . . except . . . " She looks up at me, eyes pleading. "I could have been stronger. I could have held onto it if I had just had one friend to support me. Just one friend."

I put my arms around her. "Okay," I say. "Now you do."

YOU HAVE STOLEN WHAT IS MINE. YOU BETTER WATCH YOUR BACK EVERY DAY BECAUSE I AM WATCHING YOU. WHEN I GET MY CHANCE I WILL TAKE YOU DOWN.

I stand in the hall, outside my locker, in my new jumper and gold T-shirt with my hair pulled back so beautifully, all my good feelings melting as I stare at the note. My knees shake. I lean back against the wall, clammy, nauseated, June punching at my stomach as if she wants out, and I stare at all the kids moving through the hall in all directions and wonder which one of them is trying to destroy me.

"Sophie! Come here. What are you doing way up there?"

Things are happening too fast for me. I don't understand the rules of Planet High School. When I was best friends with the captain of the basketball team, I was still an outcast. I come to a lot of games to cheer Joshua on, but I always sit high up in the bleachers by myself.

Now I've been shopping with Acacia, and I guess I'm her friend, so I'm being summoned to sit in the choicest real estate in the gym—with Acacia and Blanca Flores, and Patty Winston. Lined up behind them are Randy Torres, Greg Peterman, and Zack Maholic—three boys who just a month ago chased me through the halls like prey. Now, because Acacia, their queen, is calling me over, everyone (except Blanca, who grieves perpetually for Nestor) is smiling up in my direction, inviting me to be a golden person like them. I guess girls control the social order. Or else I'm just irresistible in my new blue jumper.

And even though the only one of them I can stand is Acacia, I hurry, tottering down the bleachers as fast as I can to accept their gracious offer. How can you turn down a promotion?

But I look into each and every face, wondering if I can see

a flicker in someone's eye that will tell me they're the crazy one who shoves notes in my locker grating. I'd been thinking it had to be a girl, but boys have access to nail polish, too. I remember Zack, chasing me and taunting me. He's always been the kind of boy I could imagine torturing animals. Even as I approach, he seems to be leering at my stomach. I turn away from him and look at Blanca, who always wears black clothes now and who keeps a handkerchief out at all times, in case a fresh wave of grief breaks out. She is such a beautiful girl, with her raven wing of black hair cupping her cheek and her eyelashes that sweep like fans when she lowers her eyes. She is almost huddled against Acacia, who holds an arm out to welcome me to her other side.

"That's it!" Acacia tells me. "You got the hair perfect tonight. Just perfect."

I fidget. June is restless, tapping and clapping her hands against me, or that's what it feels like.

"Josh says they're going to kick butt tonight," Randy says to Zack.

"If he says it, he'll do it. Josh is the man," Zack answers.

"Yeah, he can do anything," Greg agrees.

I hear something malicious in their voices. Do they mean he can get me pregnant and then make his girlfriend be nice to me? I realize how hard it must be for Acacia to be my friend, when so many people must think I'm her rival.

"I really appreciate . . . " I start to whisper, but she shushes me.

"Let's go out after the game. Just you and me and Joshua," she says. "I want to ask you something."

The three boys behind us whisper and laugh. Blanca glances over, eyelashes sweeping up and down my body. She's Acacia's best friend, clearly hurt at being excluded.

"You want to come, too?" I ask her.

Acacia elbows me. "I have something private to discuss with Sophie," she tells Blanca. "I'll call you later."

Blanca smiles a flat smile and swivels her head to the court, where the team is being introduced.

PA echoes fill the new gym, and I go back in time to the old gym and the night Nestor died. This must happen to Blanca at every game. How could it not?

I see him, body arching for a layup, rising off his toes, long black hair swirling—I can see every detail as if it were a video I could run in slow motion. Just as the ball leaves his fingers, his arms come in sharply toward his chest, both fists against his heart as if to wall out something that was trying to stab him. Still in the air, his knees bend, and he pulls into a tuck position, turning and rolling as he falls onto his left shoulder. A scream, like nothing I've ever heard from a human before—I'd almost call it a bird scream—interrupts and stops all the other sounds. No one moves. Everyone just stares at Nestor's fear-widened eyes as he makes the second sound—his last sound—a soft moan. "Oh, no."

Then Coach Haynes screams, "Call 911!" and we all come unfrozen and cell phones are beeping like crazy and everyone runs—some people toward Nestor, some away.

I am high in the bleachers, like always, and I stand up without knowing how I did it, and I see Joshua kneeling by Nestor, cradling his head and saying things to him, urging him to live. And then I look at Blanca, who is swaying on her feet, no one looking at her or helping her, and I just watch as she falls and hits her head on the bleachers.

I just watch as the paramedics come in and try to resuscitate him, but he's perfectly still. They put him on a stretcher, but they move more slowly than they did at first. I watch as the whole basketball team puts their arms around one another like a giant spider. Joshua is chanting something with them, and I realize they are praying together. A kid on the visiting team is sitting down on the gym floor, crying like a little boy.

The next day at school they tell us the news. We already know because Nestor, Blanca, and Joshua are all absent. We hear a lecture about ventricular fibrillation, and the controversy about testing young athletes to prevent this kind of thing. They say the school districts don't like to pay for it; but if we'd known, we would all have paid for it. Everyone I know would have paid anything for this not to have happened.

I wonder how Blanca can even watch a basketball game now. Or how Joshua can jump up and make a shot. He's supposed to be safe. The parents of everyone on the team had their kids screened right after it happened. But I notice Acacia picking her cuticles apart through the whole game. I hear some kind of extra rage in the cheering and booing of the guys behind us. None of us really feels safe anymore.

We order pizza with everything, because that's the way Joshua likes it. Then Acacia spends the next fifteen minutes picking all the vegetables and little pieces of meat off her slice. Joshua opens his mouth to comment on this, then shrugs, takes a handful of her discards, and scatters them over his slice.

I can't wait for all these formalities. June loves pizza and sends me signals that make me stuff it in my mouth, my whole body thrilled by the sensation of hot grease.

"Doesn't Sophie look nice?" Acacia asks Joshua. "I showed her how to do her hair."

He glances at me. "It's curlier?"

"Yeah, that's the way she is naturally." Acacia lifts a strand and drops it like a mother would do to her child.

"Nice," he says with his mouth full. "Ask her your thing, Acacia."

Acacia gives him a look, as if she wasn't quite ready to "ask me her thing," but she turns a radiant smile to me. "Sophie? Joshua and I were wondering. Would you like me to be your Lamaze coach instead of him? I mean, now that we're friends . . . "

"We've only been shopping one time!" I protest and see her

draw back. But what am I supposed to say? We're talking about me giving birth, not a lunch date. Joshua and I have all this history. I trust him. His eyes are on the table. The coward.

Silence is building up around our table like a snowfall. I'm getting madder at Joshua every minute. I asked him for something that's really important to me, and he's chickening out and . . . delegating! I suddenly realize I don't like having Acacia around every time Joshua and I are together. It's watering down our friendship. There are a million things I've wanted to talk to him about, including a little matter of a threat on my life, and I can't. Because she's always there. She's ruined my best friendship when I need it the most.

They are both staring at me now, expecting me to say more. I glare at my pizza in silence. They've ruined that, too. Now it's getting cold, and you can see the grease coagulating on it. I feel as if I could tip over the whole table!

"I don't need anybody with me," I say to my plate. June gives me a kick.

A hand touches my arm. I look up and see it's Joshua. "No, no, Sophie. It's not like that. If you want me there, I'm there. It's just that we thought . . . "

"You'd be more comfortable with another girl," Acacia finishes for him. "But I understand, Sophie. I totally understand. You don't know me that well."

"We'll do whatever you want to do," Joshua says.

I'm too confused to speak. I know they're begging me, in a way, to make it easier for them. Asking me to not put stress on their relationship by having him do something so intimate with another girl. I know he's scared silly. I also think that maybe seeing my baby born and even helping it happen might be something Acacia needs to do for herself. I wish I wasn't the one bringing so much trouble, making everything hard for everyone. Now I feel like crying. I really hate estrogen.

I finally get my brain stable enough to look up at them.

"Maybe we could decide this later," I say. "We have eight weeks. If you could both come to the classes with me, when it's closer to the time, maybe I can . . . "

"She's right," Acacia says quickly. "Of course you want to know me better."

"Let's talk about something else." Joshua picks up a limp slice of pizza and looks at it gloomily.

I scan for a topic. The things on my mind right now, like having whale hallucinations, don't seem appropriate.

"It was a good game," Acacia says lamely.

"Aaaa!" Joshua shakes his head. "We won, but we didn't play that well. The team isn't cohesive anymore."

This is such a clear reference to Nestor that it stuns us all back into silence.

"I feel sorry for Blanca," I say.

Acacia shrugs. "Some of that she does to get attention. I mean, I'm not saying she didn't love him, but some of it seems like crocodile tears to me."

I'm surprised she'd say this about her best friend.

"She's not dating anyone, though," Joshua points out.

"Well . . . that's true."

"Sometimes it feels like he's haunting that new gym," Joshua says. "Maybe because they named it for him, but I keep feeling like he's running downcourt with me, right off my left elbow. Does that sound crazy?"

Not to me, I think.

"It's all the plaques with his name and everything," Acacia says. "You see all that, and it gives a subliminal message."

"No, it's the memories," Joshua says. "The goal. It's a wonder I can even hit the goal. Every time I see it, I think about him, making that last jump."

"Let's not talk about it anymore," I say.

Joshua laughs. "We're running out of topics tonight."

Desperation makes me bold. "I've got a question. Is there a

way for me to find out who my father is? Besides asking my mother. Is there like a place on the Internet where you can search for people?"

Joshua stares at me. "Well, if you know his name, you can look him up on the Internet. You might get his e-mail and be able to contact him directly."

"But I don't know his name. That's the thing I need to get."

"What's on your birth certificate?" Acacia says.

I stare at her. "Huh?"

"She had to put a name on your birth certificate. They make the woman write something. Not that some don't lie."

"My birth certificate," I repeat like a moron. Why hadn't I ever thought of that?

"Yeah. Do you remember what it says?"

"I've never seen it!" I say. "And that's why! My God, she's shown me my baby book and my hospital bracelet—everything except a birth certificate. And that's why. His name is on it!"

"Why would she do that?" Acacia asks. "She's afraid you'll contact him? She hates him or something?"

"I don't know. There's something bad around it . . . What . . . what would a woman put down if she . . . if she didn't know the name . . . " Either June slides around or my stomach lurches, I can't tell which.

Joshua screws up his face. "What are you talking about? Your mother? She's a nice woman. She wouldn't . . . "

"I don't mean it like that," I say. I feel as if I'm betraying her by even saying these things, but I can't stop. "I had a conversation with her once that almost sounded like . . . I mean, there's a reason she won't tell me anything . . . there's something bad . . . what if some guy . . . " I can't say it.

"Attacked her?" Where would this group be, I wonder, without Acacia to finish our sentences for us?

I nod.

"Oh, Soph!" Joshua says. "You don't think that, do you?"

"I don't know," I say. "It's a possibility. There's something real bad about it or she wouldn't keep it a secret from me. It would make sense if my father was a . . . bad guy . . . and she's trying to protect me from that."

"Oh, it's not that," Joshua says. "It can't be."

"Why?" Acacia says. "You think women don't get raped?"

He flinches. "No, I know, but . . . that's so awful."

"Well," Acacia says. "Awful things happen all the time."

I look at both of them. I know from the way she says this that she hasn't told him about her abortion. She's told me something she hasn't told Joshua. That makes me feel ashamed. She trusts me, but I don't trust her.

Acacia turns to me. "I guess in a case like that the woman would write John Doe or something like that. I think she has to write something. That's how we found out who the father of my cousin's baby was. She wanted to keep it a secret, but they made her fill a name in at the hospital and then out came the whole story."

I think about that. My mother works at the hospital where June is going to be born. I'm going to have to be very careful. Because the name of June's father is not going to "come out." Not if I can help it.

"She probably keeps my birth certificate in her room somewhere," I say out loud. I'm confessing it so they can both hear it. I guess I do trust Acacia.

And it's she who gives me my absolution. "You have a right to know, Sophie."

And that's how I decide to toss my mother's room. But the question haunts me: If I have a right to know who my father is, why doesn't my mother have the right to know who the father of her granddaughter is? Well, let her find out if she can. May the best woman win.

I wake up in the middle of the night, soaking wet, words clang-

ing and banging in my brain, clamoring to be let out. I've written poems like this before—waking in an almost panic with a
load of words that boiled out of my unconscious and can't wait
to be vomited on paper. I stumble and almost knock over a chair,
scrounge on the floor for my notebook, almost upset the lamp. I
write:

Come to me
on the day of fire
the Day of the Sun
stand in the circle of grandmothers
lift your child to the fourfold embrace

A mother is a reed the wind blows through
A mother is a reed the wind blows through

Come to me
at first light
while the East wind teases the sea
while the North wind shadows our secrets
while the West wind comforts our dead

A mother is a reed the wind blows through
A mother is a reed the wind blows through

Come to me
like all the Blackbirds before you
the sacred blood has marked you
turn to the South wind with your child
give her to the strongest wind
give the strongest wind to her

A mother is a reed the wind blows through
A mother is a reed the wind blows through

I stare at the words. They just came out like that. There is nothing to look over or rewrite because I didn't write it. It was given to me, dictated from someplace outside me.

I was like a reed, with the wind blowing through.

8

My abdomen now extends 5 inches beyond my belly button. Dr. Mendez says that June weighs about 4 pounds and that if she were straightened out, she'd be about 19 inches long. My due date is in three weeks, between June first and June sixth, the same week I'll graduate from high school; but I didn't plan on going to the ceremony anyway. Dr. Mendez is happy that my blood pressure is staying low and that the spotting I had several months ago has completely stopped. We discuss the things I'm learning in Lamaze about labor and delivery, and I tell her I want a standby epidural if the pain gets bad.

"Do you have any other questions?" she asks, writing on my chart. "With a first baby it's hard to imagine what labor will be like, and that causes apprehension for some women."

I don't know what to say. I've imagined it all different ways. Sometimes I think it will be a thrill, like when you swing on a swing set and go higher than you thought you'd ever go. Sometimes I picture myself lying on a table, screaming in pain like a torture victim. "I just know that lots of other women do it, so I'll be able to do it, too" is what I choose to say. "The coolest part is that at the end, I'll see her. I can't wait to see her."

She smiles at me, woman to woman. "Yes, that is a great moment. It's also the moment when you'll be sooo glad it's over."

I laugh and watch her eyes coast up and down my chart. "Any more bad dreams? Or unusual . . . .feelings?"

I've forgotten how much I told her last time. I think I told her about the day the landscape changed right under my nose but not about the time I "traveled" from Broward county to Dade without the use of Metrorail. I picture a friendly HRS lady in the delivery room waiting to take June away from her crazy mother the minute she's born.

"No. . ." I say. "But now I'm dreaming a lot about the Tequesta Indians."

She scrunches up her face. "Who?"

Oh, well. I had been hoping there might be a common syndrome in pregnancies where the woman dreams about lost civilizations. Apparently not. "A tribe of Indians who hunted whales off Biscayne Bay."

"Oh," she says. "You've gone from whales to whale hunters. Is this something you studied in school?"

"Yes," I say. "In school."

"At least you're not dreaming about the Seminoles," she says. "Then you'd be playing bingo all night long." She closes the chart. "You're doing great, Sophie. Before you know it, we'll be meeting June in person."

I get a funny feeling when she says that. A feeling so weird I decide not to think about it at all.

I dream I'm a whale, deep in the ocean, and something is wrong with me. I know I'm too far from my pod. I've made some colossal error by straying, and now I am going into labor with no one to help me.

I'm blind, or maybe it's very dark at this depth. I can't even orient myself to know which way the surface is. I'm lost in a cold, black, watery suspension.

Labor pains come, a feeling of something stretching and contracting inside me, as if I'm a barrel swelling, threatening to break the stays. I roll in the water, roll and thrash. Some part of me knows that if my baby comes at this depth, she'll freeze to death.

My anguish comes out as a clicking sound, something like a Geiger counter. I try to swim, but my body keeps rolling, changing positions before I can get control.

Then I hear clicking coming back to me, faintly through the blackness. Many clicks, coming louder and louder.

Another seizure of pain clamps down on me, and I feel the rolling motion again. I click frantically. I know I have to find my pod, help my pod find me.

The clicking is all around me now, loud and affirmative. They are all females like me. They have done this before. They know what to do.

They bump me gently with their heads, moving me up in the water, or at least I think it's up. I hear the clicking all around me, evenly spaced. They're making a circle. I know the females will help me and my baby won't die.

Now as I roll and thrash, I feel the movement of the baby whale inside me, traveling slowly through me, a counterpoint to the now-rhythmic barrel stretching. I stop clicking and erupt into squeals of pain. The other females click steadily, trying to soothe me.

I feel something in my lower body like a sneeze would feel if you sneezed all your brains out your nose, and the water whooshes . . . That's my baby somewhere, free of my body; but I can't help her because I'm still contracting, still too confused to look for her. But I feel joyful because my baby is free.

Then I see. Half the whales have scooped up my baby, taking her to the surface with their heads, prodding her to the surface so she can breathe.

Somehow we have gotten to warmer, shallower water. I see the bright surface now, where my baby and I need to go.

My body is exhausted, but some of the females have stayed to help me, nudging and bumping me higher and higher, and then my own will takes over, and I shoot to the surface and gulp air through the back of my head.

My baby is there. I can see her little body swimming toward me as the sun dances on the water like a thousand stars, and the other females make a protective ring around us. We all sing together.

I wake up and write down the whole dream from beginning to end. In case I am cracking up, it will be useful to medical science to know what all the stages of my madness looked like.

Whatever our differences have been, my mother and I have always respected each other's privacy. If one of us gets an advertisement or a piece of junk mail, the other one is not allowed to open it. If I get a phone call, she walks out of the room, and that's trained me to do the same for her. She never comes in to "straighten" my room like some mothers I've heard about.

And so by going into her room today to try and find my father's name, I know I'm breaking an eighteen-year trust between us. That's what makes me stand in the doorway for a long time before I walk in.

Her room is so different from mine. We have matching maple-wood desks that we bought at a garage sale when I was twelve. On top of my desk right now there's a white stuffed cat, my journal, a deck of tarot cards, a heliotrope-scented candle, a heart-shaped glass bowl full of Mardi Gras beads, a coffee mug with the moon and stars on it that holds my rainbow of marking pens, my trig book, the program from Nestor's memorial service, a troll doll with purple hair wearing a ballet tutu, a picture from June's sonogram in a pink china frame, a half-eaten box of Skittles (June's newest passion), and my little purple cassette player with three tapes beside it; the *Brandenburg Concertos*, *Crucified*, the new release by I Claudius; and Roberto Pererra's *Erotica*.

On my mother's desk is a grungy-looking blotter she bought secondhand with worn-out leather edges, a brown coffee mug with yellow pencils in it, a picture of me when I was seven (when she really liked me), and a dying plant.

The first thing I do is go to her bathroom and get a glass of water for the plant. I can almost see the leaves reaching up to me, calling out, "Save us!" as I water the soil. Why did she get a plant if she doesn't want to take care of it?

I start with the desk. I know what I'm looking for. She has a flat stationery box printed with bluebells where she keeps her documents and mementos. Sometimes she brings it out to show me things: a baby picture of me, a card I made her in the second grade. But she always controls the box, taking things out and handing them to me, never letting me root through for myself. This is why I think my birth certificate, the smoking gun, is in there.

Her lap drawer has a neat stack of white envelopes, a ledger, a calculator, a checkbook and some unpaid bills, plus a stapler and a box of staples.

Top left drawer is all stationery—gifts she has hoarded over the years and used sparingly. I look through all this carefully, but the bluebell box isn't there.

The next drawer is a big one, full of photo albums and loose photos. I look carefully at all of these but don't see anyone or anything I haven't seen before. It's all pictures of me and her, not even a single picture of my grandparents, who, legend has it, kicked her out of their lives when she turned into an unwed mother. I guess I should consider myself lucky.

Trembling, I move to the nightstand. I'm hoping I can

find what I want without having to violate her closet or her dresser. I sit on the floor to avoid making an impression on the bed, feeling hot and sweaty. June is like a sack of potatoes today. I think she's angry with me for snooping around in Grandma's things. "I'm doing it for you," I tell her and pull open the drawer.

Nothing. Little packs of Kleenex, cough drops, Vicks VapoRub. Like she can't wait for her next cold. A paperback romance novel called *Creole Coquette*, which surprises me, but it's kind of comforting to see she's at least human. For fun, I open and read a paragraph:

> *Destiny paced the room, skirts flying like a wild bird flapping its wings. Her cobalt eyes flashed Creole fire, her cheeks burned like hot coals.*
>
> *"That man!" she cried as she paced faster and faster. "That dreadful man. Looking at my delicates on the washline and smiling that horrible, arrogant smile. Oh, why can't I stop thinking about it?"*

I put the book back in the drawer and close it. I sit very still on the floor, and something detonates inside me. What is it? It's like some kind of terrible sorrow or sympathy for my mom. Reading a book like this, having teenage-girl dreams about a dashing, arrogant man sweeping her off her feet. I think how lonely she must have been all these years and how lonely she'll be when June and I move out in August.

I look around her plain, spare room and wonder, Does she deny herself things to be a martyr? Or doesn't she even know how to be happy? Or was there some awful, scarring betrayal by a man that closed her down, forced her to get love in safe places, like paperback novels. And how do I know I won't end up the same? I'm planning a life just like hers, me and June against the world while I struggle through school. Will I end up reading pathetic romances while June pulls away from me and all my plants die? If I'm different, how am I different?

My self-pity hormones swell up and flow out my eyes. I've learned about these spells. You just let them pass on their own. My nose is running, and I go back to my room for a tissue. Just because I'm upset doesn't mean I'm going to do anything sloppy.

Coming back to her room, I straighten my spine and go to the closet. I try not to be overpowered by the scent of Beautiful that permeates everything and makes me feel as if she's standing right there.

She's orderly here, too. Uniforms and cardigan sweaters are on one side, on the other are the pastel jogging suits that are her uniform at home. Far to the right is her one good dress that she keeps for "just in case." Just in case a Creole man sees her underwear on the wash line. It's a nice dress, too. Black, sleeveless with a matching jacket. I've never seen it on her.

On the floor are the matching black heels, two extra pairs of nurse shoes, and several pairs of running shoes. On the closet shelf are extra handbags, an electric wok someone gave us that we never took out of the box, and . . . the stationery box with the bluebells.

I lift it down with both hands as if it were a holy relic, stepping back from a fine silt of dust that sifts down with it.

It's a big, flat box that says Forget Me Not Deluxe Stationery Set. The Forget Me Not Company is in Reading, Pennsylvania. She has tied the box shut with a blue ribbon faded almost to white.

I sit on the closet floor and untie the ribbon. My heart starts beating fast, a little girl at Christmas, hoping her father is inside the box. The first thing I see is a hankie I embroidered for her when I was in the Brownies. It says Mom with a pink blob next to it that's supposed to be a flower. Several of my stellar report cards are here and some baby pictures I've seen before and the poem I wrote that won my eighth grade literary fair's first prize; but I scrabble below that layer, like an archaeologist, digging deeper and deeper into the past. There's a lock of dark hair, not mine, but I don't know whose. There's a letter from Grandma Cooper telling Mom she's proud of the way she's doing in nursing school. Clearly, pre-me. Maybe my grandparents were like Acacia's parents: seeing a bright future for their daughter destroyed by a pregnancy. But Mom finished school, just like I'm going to. Why wouldn't they forgive and forget?

I'm thinking about that when I lift up a play program. *A Raisin In The Sun*, which kind of surprises me, since I think of Mom as a mild racist. And then, there it is. My birth certificate. Sophie Grace Cooper and her cute little footprint, born to Elizabeth Mary Cooper and Carl Wainwright.

Carl Wainwright. I'm the daughter of a man named Carl Wainwright. A real man with a real name who lives on planet Earth somewhere. I realize that up until this very moment, I've never felt I was as good as everyone else; but now I am because I have a father, too. Carl Wainwright—who could be anything from a blue-chip stock broker to a hunchback gravedigger, and I don't care. He's my father. My father. My father.

"Oh, my God!" My mother stands in the doorway looking at me as if I'm dead. "Oh, no!"

I'm not wearing a watch, but I thought I had plenty of time. Carl Wainwright's daughter often loses track of time like that. I'd been so excited a minute ago, I must not have even heard the front door open.

I struggle to my feet, still holding the paper. "I just wanted his name," I tell her. "That's all I wanted."

She's breathing so hard it scares me. "It won't do you any good. You'll never find him."

June flutters inside me, scared. "I have a right to this," I say. I want to leave the room, but I'm afraid to walk by her.

"All you've ever done in your life is destroy things." Her voice is suddenly quiet, like the mad scientist talking to James Bond.

"It's nice to hear my mother say that!" I'm hot again, sweating. "It's too bad you had to lie for all those years and pretend you loved me." My voice sounds as if I'm crying, but I'm surely not. "My baby will never feel this way! My baby . . . "

"Shut up! Shut up! Shut up!" She's screaming, putting her hands up to her ears.

My mother comes toward me, slashes her hand at the birth certificate. "Don't I have rights? Don't I have a right to privacy?"

"Not when I have a right to know," I say, sweeping it out of her reach. "Mom, I don't care if I'm illegitimate. I mean, I knew that. I just . . . "

"You just wouldn't trust me when I told you you wouldn't want to know about this. I have a right to my own life. It's not a game for you to play."

"You think this is a game to me?" Now I step toward her. "You know who your father is! You don't know what it's like not to know . . . "

"And you don't know what anything's like, because you are a stupid, naive child! You don't know what it's like when you've made a terrible mistake to try and start fresh without people digging up your past and throwing it at you!" She makes another snatch, but I'm way too fast.

"What do you mean, I don't know?" I touch my stomach. "Don't you know what I'm going through right now? Don't you remember?"

She's not listening anymore. "What did I do wrong? I didn't toss you out of the house or disown you like my parents did me! I've kept right on working to support you and take care of you no matter whose little bastard you have in there!" She points at June when she says that.

I don't have many rational thoughts after that. I remember pushing, and I remember her hitting the wall as I toss the birth certificate at her, chanting, "Carl Wainwright, Carl Wainwright, Carl Wainwright."

I remember opening my suitcase and trying to think what to take and what to leave. I try to ignore the horrible screaming and cursing coming from my bedroom doorway. She says all kinds of different sentences, but it all amounts to I hate you, I hate you, I hate you.

My anger gets colder and colder, like a stone, as I work. June holds still, afraid to move. I knew my mother hated me. I'd always known it. I'd been so careful to behave and never make her lose control like this, so I would never have to see how she really felt about me. I could even forgive that, but she called my daughter a little bastard and I will never forgive or forget that. Never.

I zip up my suitcase and sling my purse over my shoulder, trying to remember if I have any cash at all. I hobble to the door with her still screaming at me, following me down the hall, hitting me with words as if I'm a cockroach that refuses to die.

I slam the front door so hard that I lose my balance and fall; but I get up fast and start walking—the first goal is to get away from her, out of the range of her screaming. In a few more minutes, I can deal with the next problem, which is that I have absolutely nowhere to go.

9

Do nice people only come out of nice homes? I've always thought Joshua is the sweetest person I know, maybe the only person I know who I'd describe as sweet. And now that I'm living in his house, it seems as if he couldn't have turned out any other way: a cookie baked with all the right ingredients. I study his mother as I set the table, thinking she is the kind of mother I want to be for June.

Mrs. Newport (she wants me to call her Denise) is tall like her kids and has a voluptuous body: big breasts and wide hips. She likes to wear sweaters and long, swishy skirts, like the one today printed with autumn leaves. As she checks the macaroni and cheese in the oven (June's favorite dish) and leans over Joshua to correct his chopping (we all make dinner together), she is talking on the kitchen phone. She's on the phone a lot, listening more than talking: to her seventh graders, their parents, different people from her church, and seemingly anyone in distress who might cross her path. "Mmm-hmm," she says now, swishing to the stove to stir the vegetables. "Oh, I know. That's how it is. What else could you do?" She is like a priest, always blessing and forgiving everything she hears. Something in my chest aches as I watch her.

Joshua's ten-year-old sister, Kimberly, pulls me back to reality with a sharp tug on my arm. "Look what you did!" She points to the table where I have all the silverware reversed.

"Sorry." I'm already used to her bossy ways.

Done with me, she strides into the kitchen. Joshua feeds her a piece of carrot as she checks his work. Denise walks by them, flipping the phone cord up so they won't get caught in it.

"Mama!" Kimberly says. "Mama!"

Denise holds up one finger, letting the caller come to a pause. "Oh, I know. Excuse me one minute." She covers the mouthpiece. "What, sweetie?"

Kimberly rocks on her toes. "Do you want some bread or biscuits with this meal?"

"You offering to make biscuits, sweetheart? That's so nice." Her mother hugs her.

"Kiss ass," mutters Joshua.

"Booger-head!" Kimberly answers, getting a step stool to reach the Bisquick box.

I sigh, wishing I could stay forever.

When I showed up a week ago, Mrs. Newport—Denise— called my mother immediately. I assumed that meant I was going to be sent back home and was already laying plans as I sat at her kitchen table, playing with the zipper on my suitcase.

"Ms. Cooper? How are you; this is Denise Newport, Joshua's mother. I wanted you to know right away that Sophie is here, safe and sound."

I felt my face get hot. Meanwhile, Kimberly had sidled up and was staring at me with her arms folded. Joshua stood in the doorway, looking nervous.

"Oh, well, Ms. Cooper, mothers and daughters have been having words since time began and I suppose—how's that? No, of course she didn't tell me anything, and I wouldn't ask her—

or you. I'm just calling to tell you your girl is in a safe place, and we'll take good care of her until you work it out."

"No!" I said. "I'm getting my own place."

She didn't seem to hear me.

"When will your baby come?" Kimberly asked. She had eyes like a little owl.

"In June. That's her name, too. June."

"A girl?" Kimberly smiled. "If I had a baby, I'd want it to be a girl, too."

"Oh!" Her mother covered the receiver. "What did I hear you say? What are you thinking about fifteen years too soon?"

Kimberly giggled. "I meant later, Mama. After I finish my education."

"And get married," Joshua reminded her. Then he looked at me and ducked his head as if he thought he'd insulted me.

"Can I put my hand on it?" Kimberly asked in the shyest voice I'd ever heard from her.

"Sure." Everybody wants to do that. Most people don't bother to ask and it's creepy, but not with a little kid like Kimberly.

Gingerly she put her hand out and rested it lightly on top of my abdomen. I wished June would move, but she was being quiet.

Kimberly smiled and then leaned over and put her ear where her hand had been. "Oh!" she jumped up, surprised.

"Baby's telling you to mind your own business," Joshua told her.

Kimberly covered her mouth with both hands. Her eyes were huge. "It sounded like the ocean!"

We have pork chops, macaroni and cheese, tossed salad, biscuits, and green beans for dinner. For dessert there's butter pecan ice cream. I can practically hear June wondering why I don't feed her like this all the time.

After dinner we all do homework at the kitchen table, including Denise, who has a lesson plan to prepare on women writers. Every once in a while she throws out a name to see if we know what the woman has written. At eight o'clock Denise takes a bath, Joshua goes outside to practice hoops and Kimberly and I watch *Gilmore Girls*. At nine Kimberly takes her bath, and Joshua gets his turn with the TV, which turns out to be the second half of *Smackdown!* Denise reads a book and shakes her head from time to time to let Joshua know she doesn't like wrestling, but she lets him watch.

They put me in a guest room with flowered sheets and a picture of a tiger on the wall. I had been the last one to take a bath (Joshua takes showers), and as I lay in bed, I can smell warm waves of soap-perfume coming off my body. I hear Joshua through the wall, talking on the phone to Acacia, the bass from his stereo thumping like a heartbeat.

I think of Saturday, when I have to try and find a job and a place to live as fast as I can. But that's two days off. Tonight I'm one of Denise Newport's children: warm, safe, and loved.

I sleep soundly with no dreams.

By the time I look at the third apartment, it isn't fun anymore. The first apartment was on the seventh floor of a mid-rise with no elevator. No air-conditioning either. "When you're up this high, the breeze from the window keeps it cool," says Mr. Scalla, the landlord. He has trouble getting the window open to show me. "Because I just painted," he explains. "I always put in fresh paint for every new tenant. Not everyone will do that for you." He pounds the window frame with both hands to loosen the paint. A shower of silverfish tumble at our feet, like a Las Vegas jackpot. "That's because I just had pest control in here," Mr. Scalla explains. "You can see they're all dead."

☆

The second apartment isn't bad, but the landlord is. "Boyfriend run out on you?" he asks my stomach. "When will you girls ever learn?" Then he winks at me. "Not that we guys want you to. Hey, what's the matter? Did I say something? Where you going? Hey!"

Between my second and third apartments, I have a job interview. I am responding to an ad that says, "APPOINTMENT SETTERS. FLEX HRS. NO EXPER. WILL TRAIN. $10 PER HR."

I find out "appointment setter" means "phone solicitor." My potential boss, Jack Platt, shows me a script.

HELLO, MRS.   , THIS IS   FROM THE MAGAZINE COMPANY.

"The magazine company?" I ask. "That's our name?"

"We don't have a name," Jack Platt says. "We're a conduit. If they ask, you say, 'The company that sends you all your magazines'"

I frown and read farther.

THIS IS A COURTESY CALL TO THANK YOU FOR BEING SUCH A GOOD CUSTOMER AND TO LET YOU KNOW THAT A SELECT FEW, LIKE YOURSELF, ARE NOW ENTITLED TO SIXTY ISSUES OF   MAGAZINE. OKAY?

"Sixty issues," I say. "That's five years! You're giving away five-year subscriptions?"

"No, sending. We're sending. We ask them about method of payment later in the script. After they say 'okay'. Okay?"

I feel as if I'm going to throw up, and it's not the baby. "To thank them for being a good customer, you stick them with a five-year magazine subscription?"

Jack Platt, who looks as if he is just biding time until he gets a chance to act or model, blinks at me. "They can say no if they want to."

I stand up. "So can I."

The world, I'm learning in just one day, is harder than I thought.

Joshua and Acacia meet me for a Coke at five o'clock. It takes me five minutes to pry my shoes off my swollen feet.

"You look tired," Joshua says. "How'd it go?"

I try to find a position in the chair that doesn't hurt my spine. "I still don't have a job, I still don't have an apartment, I have a blister on the back of my heel, and my homework isn't done."

"You're trying too hard," Joshua says. "Anyway, you can stay with us as long as you want. Mom loves you."

Acacia puts her hand over mine. "I wish you could stay with me," she says. "But my parents . . . aren't cool."

"I know." She doesn't have to tell me what kind of feelings an unwed mother would stir up over there.

"Joshua has something he wants to ask you." Acacia's eyes sparkle with mischief.

"I won't marry you," I tell him, and we all laugh.

"She'll say no to this," Joshua says. "Just watch."

"Ask her!" says Acacia.

Joshua giggles. "I'm afraid for my life."

"Just ask me!" I hate suspense.

He can hardly get out the words. "Do you want to go to the prom with us?"

I crack up, too, thinking of myself in a Cinderella dress, only in my case the pumpkin is under the skirt. "You're both asking me?"

Acacia grins. "Yes. Joshua asked me, and I said, 'Why can't Sophie come, too?' We'll have fun."

"No, thanks," I laugh. "I've seen *Carrie*. But you guys are so sweet to think of me. I really appreciate . . . "

"No!" Acacia slaps my hand gently. "You're not taking me seriously. We mean it. We'll do the whole bit: get a limo . . . drink ginger ale out of champagne glasses. . . . If you're there, Joshua won't want to drink and get evil ideas."

"Oh, so that's it," he says.

"What am I supposed to wear, Fairy Godmother? Something from the Mommy Prommy Boutique? I really don't think I should invest in a maternity formal."

"Gotcha covered. My fat cousin Tanya says you can borrow a formal from her. If you can fill up the cups, we're in business."

Joshua puts his hands over his ears. "And she wonders where I get evil ideas!"

"You just leave it to me," Acacia tells me. "I am your fairy godmother."

Maybe she is. All I know is that for the first time that day, I don't feel like an old, fat woman whose feet hurt and who has to sell magazines and go home to an apartment full of silverfish. I feel like a kid again, somebody who can still have fun. I guess that's all friends can really do for you in the long run.

I finally finish my homework and put down my pen. I study Reid's profile as he stabs the computer keys. He's mad because I just broke up with him.

"I'm having a baby," I tell him, picking up where we left off an hour ago. "You think I can raise a child and go to college on babysitting money?"

He shrugs, the thirteen-year-old's answer to everything, and keeps stabbing keys. I can't understand what he's doing, playing some kind of computer game where he goes through tunnels and scary things pop out at him.

"You don't even need a babysitter anymore. If I wasn't here

you could have your friends over and trash the place."

He enters some kind of information, and the little wizard in front of him blows up in a cloud of dust. "I don't have any friends."

I wonder if that's true. I hate to hear him say that. Until I met Joshua, I was like that: bouncing between being totally ignored by other kids and being outright picked on. Maybe "only" children have a handicap, don't know how to play the game until it's too late. Since Reid's a boy, I figure it's even worse for him. Maybe other boys beat him up. He's not very big. Because he's my friend, I've never looked at him objectively, but I can see with his flinching mannerisms and his big vocabulary, he's a juicy target for mean kids.

"I'm your friend," I say.

He pounds the keys. "Till when?"

"Always, Reid. It's just going to change. I need a better job. I have to find an apartment. I can't stand what I'm doing now, sponging off everybody. And in the fall I'll have college and a new baby."

"Yeah. I can see how you'll fit me into all that. Look, don't lie to me. You'll never have time to do more than send me a birthday card. Just tell the truth."

I'm trying to think of the right answer when he whirls around, staring at me, and blurts, "If I was just a little older, I'd marry you!"

Then he turns back around, head down, shoulders heaving. I don't know if he's panting or crying. On the screen the character who is supposed to be him is getting slowly eaten by a dragon: chomp, chomp, chomp.

"Reid. That's the nicest thing anyone ever said to me."

The breathing slows, deepens. He shrugs again. I wait awhile, letting him recover.

"Reid? Would you help me do something that's really important to me?"

He nods. I figure he'd do anything for me, blow up the Capitol Building if I asked. "Is there a way to find people on the Internet?"

He looks around. "A couple of ways. Is this about the whales and the Indians?"

I laugh. "No, this is about my father. I found out my father's name, and I want to look for him. Can I do that?"

"We can try." He wipes out the dungeon and brings up his home page. "The easiest way is to search for an e-mail address." His fingers fly, and screens start changing, from his home page to the place he keeps the addresses of all his anonymous friends. He clicks a box that says, LOOK UP. That takes him to a screen covered with question marks that says, WHO? WHERE?

"Your father?" Reid says. "Really?"

"Really." My voice breaks a little. "Carl Wainwright."

He types the name in a box. I lean forward to look at it. He chooses all matches.

Choices flood the screen. Names and e-mail addresses. I vow never to be part of the internet and have so little privacy. We scroll through names, but none are close enough. CHARLES WANGER, CARL BOOKWRIGHT, CAL WANSBARGER.

"Garbage," Reid concludes. "Either he doesn't have e-mail or he has a server that guards his address. But don't give up the ship."

He opens his home page again and chooses SEARCH which shows a pair of binoculars.

"If he ever did anything interesting, or if he has a Web site, he'll come up here." The button is pushed.

Two matches are found. "Don't get excited yet," Reid says. He clicks on the first match, headed WINSTON CUP, 2000.

I come up next to him, peering at the press release that appears, trying to imagine my dad, the race car driver.

But Reid is way ahead of me. "No. See? There's a Carl Gunderson, and then later there's a Bob Wainwright driving a different car. My browser just matches words."

"Stupid browser," I say, picturing a little animal, like a badger, digging into the wrong hole.

Reid chooses the second match to my father's name, headed, ominously, MEMORIAL FUND.

I get a sudden cold feeling as the article pops up.

CREATED TO HONOR THE CONTRIBUTIONS OF THE LATE CARL WAINWRIGHT TO LEARNING AND LITERACY. CONTACT PALM BEACH COUNTY LIBRARY FOR DETAILS. A NONPROFIT FUND USED TO PURCHASE ALA BOOKS FOR RELUCTANT READERS FOR THE LIBRARY SYSTEM.

"My mom went to college in Palm Beach County," I say. "It could be him."

"Or his son!" Reid says eagerly, obviously trying to hold back the tears he sees in my eyes. "Or no connection at all. Your father could be some totally other Carl Wainwright who never read a book in his life."

"Or my father could be this dead guy who was dedicated to language and literacy. English is my best subject, Reid. I want to be a writer."

Reid sighs. He seems to feel bad he's delivered me a dead father. "Are you going to call the library and ask about him? If they send you a brochure about the fund, it will tell all about him probably."

"I don't know." I'm suddenly tired. "Turn it off."

The screen and the room go dark. Reid and I just sit there and listen to each other breathe. I think to myself how much alike we are. At a time like this, neither one of us has a clue what to say, or even the wherewithal to turn on a light.

"You're quiet tonight," Mike says, as he drives me back to Joshua's house.

"Reid and I had an intense night," I tell him. "For

instance, he asked me to marry him."

"That's pretty chivalrous," Mike says. "Actually, I think he's in love with you."

"I know," I say. "But he's totally nice about it. You know what I mean?"

"Yeah. Actually, Sophie, I was thinking about making a chivalrous offer to you myself."

I look over, startled. "Mike, I'm only eighteen, and you must be . . . "

"No! No! NO!" He laughs. "Although after tonight I guess I'm still single."

Reid had told me there was trouble with the Donkey. "You broke up with your girlfriend?"

"Not formally, but I think we're just about there. You know the stage where you both take everything the other one says wrong."

I say "yes," but actually I know nothing about the stages of relationships, since I've never had one.

He sighs. "Anyway, I think I'm looking at staying single for a while longer, and I keep thinking how good it would be, with the hours I work, to have some real help."

It's ten-thirty at night, but suddenly I feel as if the sun is coming up. "Like an au pair?"

"Exactly. Think how perfect, Sophie. You need a place to stay. I have a three-bedroom house. Reid adores you. You can go to school and have a job with flexible hours. I'll never have to dust that frigging coffee table again. It's a win-win."

"Are you just saying this to help me out?"

"No! Right now, I'm paying a fortune for a cleaning lady and a fortune for take-out food, and I pay you to babysit. This is just smart consolidation."

"Does it look all right?" I ask, feeling like a dumb teenager. "And what about the baby? Are you okay with having a baby in the house?"

"I think we can make it work, and I don't care what people think. Do you?"

"No. I gave up on that around nine months ago."

He laughs. "It would be cool, Sophie. Reid could babysit for you sometimes. Like karma."

I see a lot of things wrong with it. I'd be back in my old neighborhood within harassing distance of my mother. Maybe it would be bad for Reid to have to live with an older girl he's got a crush on. Maybe Mike doesn't remember what little babies are like.

But I think of his nice, comfortable house and how Reid needs a friend who understands him, and I picture trying to go to college and work as a phone solicitor and live in a silverfish apartment with a tiny baby all by myself. All in all, this sounds like the best offer I could possibly get. Unless I turn out to inherit a million from the estate of Carl Wainwright.

I slump back in my seat and gaze at the moon. "You got yourself a deal."

10

I've always loved the water, even before June came to me and brought me these strange dreams and visions. Last summer Joshua and I went to the beach almost every day, and we would take turns swimming in the ocean. I always liked to swim out beyond the point of safety, where the water turns cold and you can't put your feet down, where you feel mysterious currents and tides pulling beneath the surface. Where weird creatures brush against you and make you swim away fast, heart pounding, like a little kid. A few times I've actually felt rip currents. They drag you out when you try to swim back to shore. It's terrifying, but the trick, as every Florida kid knows, is to relax and swim parallel to the shore until you're out of that little pocket of madness, then you can get control again.

I love all that the way I love roller coasters or anything that simulates danger. It's fun to get flooded with adrenaline, feel your heart pound, but know at the same time you're safe, the danger is temporary.

But now I feel as if I'm in danger all the time, and it isn't fun anymore. I feel as if I'm hurtling through space, on a collision course with something that will splinter me into a cloud of atoms.

I'm too far from shore, beyond the curve of the horizon. June has taken over my body, my mind, my whole destiny. I've lost my mother, my home, the future that an A student should expect. I eat what June wants, think her thoughts, dream her dreams.

I read everything I can find on the Tequesta Indians and whales, trying to make out what June is trying to tell me. I go to the Bible and read the story of Jonah. I read it several times.

I try to study for finals, and suddenly I'm standing in front of Mike Sullivan's linen closet, pulling out a quilt and spreading it on the bed in my guest room. I have to have it, have to wander the house taking other things, like a bird building a nest. The little watercolor picture in the second bathroom. A basket that holds nails in the garage, which June makes me fill with seashells. Mike buys a crib for me, and it makes me cry because Mom has my crib saved in storage, sitting all alone. But once I get the crib, June takes over again, forcing me to spend one whole day making a mobile of tropical fish.

At two a.m. she will wake me up to bump against Mike's furniture in the dark, lumbering into the kitchen to claw at a loaf of bread and gouge a stick of butter, or rummage like a bear in the pantry closet, searching for tomato soup. The worst thing is potato chip cereal. She makes me crush potato chips in a bowl, pour milk on it, shake salt over it and gobble it with a spoon. The mornings after these night raids I feel ashamed, as if I were out all night having some kind of wild, forbidden sex.

The dreams are in technicolor now, with booming quadraphonic sound. Sometimes I'm a whale, and I see a man swimming toward me, trying to climb on my back. I know he is a whale hunter and that he will ride me and suffocate me. Sometimes my pod comes to rescue me and drive him off, but other times I'm alone, and he catches me, and I wake up with the blood pounding in my ears, holding the edge of the bed to keep me rooted in the here and now.

I get four A's and two B's on my final exams. My poem on Persephone takes first prize in the literary fair. Joshua gives his class ring to Acacia. My mother doesn't call.

On Memorial Day I pick wildflowers and take them to the cemetery where Nestor Chanate is buried. I'm surprised to see how neglected the grave is, no one but me has brought flowers. I had half hoped to run into Mrs. Chanate. I guess that's how desperate for mothers I am now.

I think about my father, Carl Wainwright, but I can't make myself do anything. I know I could call the foundation and probably get a brochure with a picture, or I could look him up in the library now and find all kinds of articles. But what difference does it make? He's dead. I'm just as fatherless as I was before. My mother was right, for once. I didn't want to know this.

I have what will probably be my last visit to Dr. Mendez. I tell her I'm scared because June doesn't move and because I have cramps sometimes. But she says June can't move so much anymore because she's filling up the whole space. She says when I have cramps to lie down and take it easy, but that at this point, it's not anything to worry about. Dr. Mendez asks about my mother. I tell her the truth, that we're not speaking. She asks about my mental state, and I lie, saying I am just fine.

It's June. The prom is three days away, graduation seven. Same as my due date. At this point I just want to lie in bed, but I have to go through with the prom because Acacia is trying so hard to do something nice for me, and I owe her.

It's amazing how well-designed prom dresses are for pregnant bodies. It makes you wonder. Acacia and Joshua came over an hour ago—Acacia with two garment bags full of fat cousin Tanya's formals and a shopping bag of accessories. Joshua brought a boom box and his mother's digital camera. We're playing fashion show.

Joshua and Acacia sit on Mike's couch—well, I guess it's my couch now, too. Back in my new bedroom/nursery, I have Tanya's astonishing wardrobe spread out. It looks as if a whole ice-cream store has exploded. Draped over the crib are swirls of lemon custard satin and a double scoop of pistachio chiffon. On the bed where June and I sleep are puddles of raspberry, watermelon, and grape. What kind of life does Tanya lead, I wonder, that she has collected this sea of formals? I carefully load myself into a vanilla frappé with sprinkles, arch my back to pull up the zipper, adjust my baby-enhanced cleavage, and carefully pouf out the skirt to drape over my upside-down papoose.

I throw open the door and saunter down the hall to the runway—three beach towels laid end to end on the living-room floor. Joshua presses Play, and "I'm Too Sexy" comes thumping and bumping into the room. Acacia calls out Jerry Springer phrases and takes pictures. Sophie the Fertility Goddess in aqua, in flaming orange, in the black dress with the rose on the hip that I love but that Acacia says would be bad luck.

"Go on, girl! Whooooo!" Acacia screams, as I hold out my vanilla skirt and spin on bare feet. "Work it, honey! Strike a pose. Sell it to me, baby, make me buy it."

I cooperate, turning and jutting, thrusting out my stomach, crossing my eyes, making the three-point crab. Joshua is doubled over, laughing.

The front door opens, and we all jump, as if we've been caught in a drunken orgy. But it's just Reid, home from school. He stares at me in my big vanilla dress, forgetting to close the front door. Slowly his backpack slips off his shoulder and goes thunk at his feet.

"Hi, sweetie, come to the fashion show!" Acacia pats the

couch next to her. "We're dressing up Cinderella for the ball."

Reid begins to blush. It comes up out of his neck and goes all the way to the roots of his hair. "You look like a queen," he says to me.

"A drag queen!" Joshua screams. Acacia smacks him, but I laugh.

"Look at the pictures on the coffee table," I tell Reid, who is having trouble getting unfrozen. "Those are the dresses you missed."

He walks over and picks up pictures. "Damn," he says.

I laugh, closing the front door and picking up his backpack. "I guess you like them all. Tell me what you think of the black one."

"It's nice . . . don't wear that to a prom, though."

"See?" Acacia says. "Even a baby knows."

"Okay, get comfortable, Reid." I turn to go back down the hall. "We've got about a hundred dresses to go."

"All right!" he says.

I love that kid. I might marry him in ten years, when I'm twenty-eight and he's twenty-three. I shuck off my vanilla dress and survey the rest of the rainbow. There's one I've been sort of drawn to but afraid of, all at the same time. It's blood-red, ruby red, Dorothy's-shoes red. I never wear that color, but I'm always drawn to it. It's too sexy for even a prom dress, really. Strapless, with a sparkly beaded top and a taffeta skirt with little weights sewn in the hem. When I put it on, I see why. They make the skirt whirl and twirl around my ankles like Ginger Rogers. In the mirror I'm an overblown gladiola, a pregnant laser show, a priestess of wine and blood. I think of Persephone. I lean closer to the mirror and see how the color transforms my face into something pure and glowing, makes my hair look dark and burnished, lights up the dark green of my eyes. I look exotic, foreign. I'm beautiful. I'm terrible. I'm a glamorous, ethereal nightmare flower. I know this dress has tapped into the real me, a person I've never seen before. A person I haven't quite become. This is the dress I want to wear to the prom, to say good-bye to high school and celebrate all the wonderful, horrible things that have happened to me there.

I open the door and walk slowly. I walk differently in this dress. I know I have a different expression from before. Joshua forgets to start the music. Acacia doesn't take any pictures. They all stare at the power the red dress has unleashed.

"You can't wear that one," Joshua says finally.

"No," Acacia says softly. "She has to."

Later I am back in my blue jumper, tearing up romaine. Reid sits at the kitchen table, doing his homework. Mike will be home in about an hour. I feel peaceful, like a married woman, fixing dinner for the family. Reid is no longer my fiancé; he's my son, and I have another baby on the way. I fork the potatoes, even though I know they aren't done yet, just to touch them. I hope I can live in this house forever.

The doorbell rings. Reid and I look at each other. He slides off his chair and goes to answer.

I feel June squirming around in her tight space. I pat her. "Want out? It won't be long now."

Reid comes back holding a white envelope.

"There was nobody out there," he says. "Just this." His hand trembles. A TV addict like Reid knows perfectly well what those magazine letters, spelling SOPHIE, mean.

I take the envelope and open it, turning away to read so he can't see my face.

ON AND ON YOU GO USING PEOPLE AND TAKE WHAT YOU WANT. YOU WHORE NOW YOU MOVE IN WITH A MAN AND PROBABLY WILL MOLEST HIS KID TO. YOU WHORE YOU WHORE YOU WHORE. YOUR TIME WILL COME WHEN I CAN FIND YOU ALONE AND I

WILL HURT YOU LIKE YOU HURT SO MANY PEOPLE
ESPECIALLY ME. NOW I JUST LIVE TO GET REVENGE
ON YOU SOPHIE AND I WILL. REMEMBER WHAT THE
WITCH SAID TO DOROTHY YOU THINK YOUR SAFE
WITH YOUR FRIENDS AROUND YOU BUT THEY WONT
ALWAYS BE AROUND. I AM THE WITCH AND I WILL
GET YOU MY PRETTY. AND THAT GOES FOR YOUR
LITTLE BASTARD BABY TO.

My hands shake so hard, the paper tears. I see sparkly
things at the edge of my field of vision. Reid rushes forward,
grabs me as if he thought I was going to fall.

"Let me see."

I hold it away from him. "No, I don't want you to see it." I
tear it in halves, in quarters, in sixteenths, in thirty-seconds. I
tear and tear and tear. Little pieces of hate confetti fall on the
kitchen floor. Tears are running down my face. I think I know
who it is. I think I've always known.

Reid is staring at me, hands out, as if I'm falling and he has
to be ready to catch me. "All I want to do is live my life!" I shout
at the paper bits. "Why can't people just leave me alone? Why
do I have to pay for every single. . ."

"Give me those." He makes a grab. I swirl my hands away,
ticker tape flying in an arc. How will we ever sweep it all up? I
start to cry hard because I can't protect Reid from this. You can't
protect anybody from anything. Everything always comes out. I
sob; I wail. My hands fall to my sides, and the rest of the letter
showers down on the floor. I'm a curse on this house. A plague.

Reid turns off the stove, where the potatoes are boiling
over. Watching me carefully, he goes to get the dustpan.

The night of the prom I have this backache like nothing I've ever felt in my life, like a fist is gripping my ovaries and trying to twist them. I can't concentrate, and I drop my earrings three times before I get them through my earlobes.

I stare with dread at fat cousin Tanya's sparkly, red, spike-heel pumps, which seem to be sneering at me from the gloom of the closet. Why am I doing this? I'm a week from delivery. I'm tired. I want to lie down on my bed and tell Mike and Reid to order me a couple of Meat Lovers pizzas for when I wake up.

But I have to go. Acacia has rented a limo, and she and Joshua have gone to so much trouble trying to make me happy. I have to at least pretend to go along with it. Next week, if I go into labor, I'll need my coaches. This is the least I can do for them.

Anyway, since I'm not going to graduation, this is my chance to say good-bye to high school. The place where I went from the most invisible girl to the most visible one in nine short months. The place where I've met the kindest and the cruelest people I've ever known. The place where Mr. Kissanis helped me find my calling to be a poet. The place where Nestor Chanate died. The place where my baby was conceived. The place where someone is threatening to kill me.

I finally got the courage to ask Acacia for one of her dark lipsticks. She gave me something called Origins Liquid Lip Glaze in a color called Caramel Candy, which you'd think would be brown, but on my mouth it's like garnet. It harmonizes so well with the color of my dress, it makes me realize Acacia is some kind of artistic genius.

Then I turn again to face the shoes. I've always felt that if you're going to do something, you should do it all the way. I hoist up my weighted skirt and step up into the shoes.

My back screams in pain. I stumble out of the pumps as if they'd burned me, almost twisting my ankle in the process; but the back pain won't stop. I double over, breathing hard. I realize that the pain had faded for a while, but now it's back like a tidal wave. Against my will a little sound comes out of my mouth, a wussy little mew, like a kitten out in the rain.

Then the pain eases up. Spooked, I slowly straighten my back. Weird. I guess it hurts June for me to point my toes that way; maybe it shifts her into an uncomfortable position. Whatever the reason, I have a full-blown phobia for the shoes now. I scan the closet in despair: brown sandals, black flats I know Acacia will hate, and my six pairs of Keds. One of them is red, almost a perfect match to the dress. It seems like the only thing to do, and the idea makes me happy. Before, I would have been completely in costume. Now there's a little element of the real me, peeking out from under the hem of my dress.

In the living room, Mike and Reid are watching TV, but they both stand up when they see me, as if my dress is playing the national anthem.

"You look incredible," Mike says. "I wish I was ten years younger."

"I wish I was ten years older!" Reid says. He is openly staring.

"I feel awful," I say. "I think it's a little too close to the due date for me to go out dancing."

"Reid has something for you," Mike prompts.

Reid is still busy staring.

"Reid!"

"Oh, yeah, wait right here." Reid runs back to the kitchen and opens the refrigerator.

I screw up my face. Do they think I want a snack at a time like this?

But when he comes out with the little box in both hands, I realize what it is. The kid I babysit for has bought me a corsage. It's perfect, too, a white orchid, dotted with ruby red.

"Don't let Reid put it on you." Mike chuckles.

"I wasn't going to!" Reid blushes furiously.

I pin it into my hair, since there's no place else to put it.

"There," says Mike. "Now you're perfect."

"Not quite." I lift my dress and show them my shoes.

They both crack up. "Perfect in case you need to make a quick getaway," Mike says.

The doorbell rings. It's Joshua, in his tux, who is maybe the handsomest man I've ever seen, and Acacia who has a molded, sparkly white dress with a big slit up the side and a white rose on her wrist.

"Wow!" I say. "We're all gorgeous!"

Mike gets the camera, and we take a lot of pictures, some serious and some silly, such as one of Reid, playing Prince Charming, putting the sneaker on my foot. I'm completely happy and notice that my backache is gone.

We get more hilarious in the limo: a campy powder blue job with a fishtail. We're like kids at a slumber party, giggling at stuff that isn't funny, spilling nonalcoholic champagne on our expensive clothes, making the driver warn us three times to settle down.

The theme of the prom is Paradise Lost. This translates into paper palm trees, obscene-looking flower arrangements, and a DJ playing things such as "She Runs Away" and "La Isla Bonita."

Everyone is dancing, even the nerds, and we're swept with searchlights of stardust and color. There's a group feeling of letting out, letting go, going crazy in the happiest possible way.

Like the joke people were reciting all last week: "Why do we go to high school?" Answer: "Because it feels so good when it stops."

The DJ puts on a song I like, Morphine's "Rope on Fire," and all three of us—Joshua, Acacia and me—start moving and swaying. The song has this East Indian twang that makes you think of a cobra coming out of a basket. Joshua and Acacia begin to undulate, reaching up to join their hands in the air. "Do you mind if we dance?" Acacia calls to me. I shake my head "no," showing with a smile how much I love their love.

Even though I have no partner, the song won't let me go, and I undulate alone. I don't care if my belly is huge or if my blood-red dress sticks out like a sore thumb or even if I look crazy, dancing all by myself. It's between my body and the music—nothing else is important.

I close my eyes for a second, and when I open them, Mr. Kissanis is in front of me, dancing as my partner. I'm startled at first, then worried about how this looks for him; but it was his choice to come over, and I refuse to break the spell of how I feel because of what someone might think.

Of all the people I've met in these four years, Mr. Kissanis did the most for me. He showed me books I couldn't have found for myself, such as *Mother of Pearl* and *White Oleander*. He told me I had talent, and he started studying poetic technique so he could help me jump from level to level. He showed me a way that I could be special.

The song changes to Rusted Root's "Virtual Reality," a really fast number. I'm amazed at how agile and unpregnant

I feel and what a good dancer he is, despite his age.

"Great dress," he pants.

"Thanks! I have to get it back to the fat lady at the opera by ten!"

He laughs. "When are you due?" He has to shout over the rising tide of the music.

"Any minute now with a song like this!" I think I'm bordering on some kind of ecstasy, sweating and working my muscles, getting exhausted like children do when they play hard, suspending a whole year of doubts and questions in one big explosion of music and colored lights. When I look up at the ceiling, I see galaxies being born. When I look down at the swirl of my red skirt, it's as if I'm being swallowed by a flower.

The song ends. Mr. Kissanis puts his arm around me and walks me to a table. "Congratulations on the poetry contest," he says.

"I wouldn't be in it if it wasn't for you," I tell him.

He grins like a little boy. "Want something to drink?" He looks around and loses his smile. I follow his sight line to Mrs. Kissanis, glaring at him from a far corner. I don't blame her either. I'd do the same with my husband if I had one.

"I gotta go." He lays his hand over mine. "Listen, Sophie, would you drop me a note from time to time after you graduate? I don't want to lose touch with you. I think you're going to be published someday, and it's probably the only shot at reflected glory I'll ever have—being able to say I was your teacher."

"Sure." I pat my stomach. "I'll let you know how the baby turns out, too."

"Oh yeah," he laughs nervously. "Sure." He scurries off to his wife. I watch them reenact the myth of Zeus and Hera that he taught me about.

The song changes to Monica's "Just Another Girl." Joshua and Acacia appear with plastic cups of 7UP in hand, and we chug in unison. "You guys make a cute couple out on the dance floor," I say.

"So do you and June," says Joshua.

Acacia plops in a chair and pulls off her shoes. "Wish I'd worn my Keds," she says. "Joshua. Ask Sophie to dance. I'm puttin' my feet up." She literally props them on the table. The slit in her skirt waterfalls open.

"Hey!" Joshua bends down, frantically trying to close the gap. "What's the matter with you? Don't be showing my cookies to the whole room!"

She works her fingers into his hair. "For your information, baby, they're my cookies, and I promise to keep my legs down if you'll dance with Sophie."

The song changes to David Gray's "Babylon." We merge out onto the floor, taking a few seconds to find a rhythm with each other. It's fun, but we both keep an eye on Acacia, who waves, blows kisses, and threatens to prop her legs up again. We also see that when Anthony Batiste, captain of the football team, approaches her, she waves him off with a sweet smile, pointing to Joshua.

The exertion is catching up with me now. Halfway through the song I really want to sit down, but I resolve to stick it out, grateful to God for the tennis shoes.

Then something really bad happens. I suddenly realize I feel kind of wet down there, like when you forget to change a tampon. I start to panic, remembering the bleeding I had in the first few months. With a baby it could be anything; maybe I've reached a point where I can't control my bladder. Then I realize I'm a week from my due date, and this could be my water breaking! I grab Joshua's arm so hard he cries out. "I have to go to the bathroom!" I hiss.

He throws up his hands in surrender. "Okay! I won't try to stop you!" He starts back to Acacia, and I hear him say, "Hormones!" to himself.

I fight my way through the dancing crowd. Light swooshes in my face and blinds me. I get to the hallway outside the gym, where the bathroom is, and there's a line. I feel very wet now, and I want so much to just lift up my dress in front of everyone and see if it's blood or water, if my baby is being born or dying. For a minute I'm paralyzed, and I find myself staring at Nestor's memorial plaque hanging over the gym door, reminding me that terrible disasters happen all the time.

Then I come to life and take off, holding up my hem, very, very grateful to God for the tennis shoes. The next nearest bathroom is by the art room, down a long corridor to my left. No lights are on and it's totally dark, but at least in this bathroom, if it's not locked, I'll have some privacy. Liquid is starting to trickle down my leg.

"Oh, please," I whisper, the best prayer I can manage.

I feel for the door and push it open, grope for the light switch and turn it on, feel for my underwear and pull it down. It's clear. It's amniotic fluid. I'm going to have my baby.

Then I double over as the backache starts again, and I think, You idiot! It was labor pains! What good are the childbirth classes if you're too dumb to recognize labor when it happens? But they told us it would be like cramps, not a pain in the back . . . I hope this doesn't mean something's wrong.

I try to think. When was the last one? When I was getting dressed. It must have been around six-thirty. I don't have a watch, but I figure it's eight or eight-thirty now. So the pains are far apart. That's good. But they also told us when the water breaks, the baby could be imminent, so how do I put that together? Meanwhile I'm holding my dress up with my panties around my knees, crab-walking into a stall and wrapping toilet paper around my hand to blot up all the fluid.

I need help, I think. I could pass out here. I decide to buy a pad from the machine, in case I've got a gusher coming; and

111

then I'll just have to get myself back down that dark corridor to the gym, find my coaches, and get us all to the hospital, where I can demand every kind of painkiller they have, since it feels as if June is trying to burst out of my lower back instead of come the right way.

I fumble in my useless little bag for a quarter and put it in the Kotex machine. It doesn't work. Something snaps, and I pound the metal box with my hands, screaming curses. The pain is sawing through me. Why does it last so long? I thought early labor pains were short. Didn't they teach me anything I could use?

Okay, Sophie, focus. Don't worry about dribbling on the floor. People will understand. I put myself back together as best I can and start to hobble toward the bathroom door when it flies open, crashing into the wall.

Out of the darkness comes Blanca Flores, thin as an umbrella in her black dress, gliding into the light, burning me with her eyes. "Thank you, Sophie," she says softly, opening her purse. "I don't know what made you come down here, so far from everyone, but thank you." She takes out some kind of long kitchen knife, like you'd use to filet a whole salmon. "You made this much, much easier for me."

12

"Blanca," I say, trying to think while June sends me a pain that flashes lights in my head. "You're making a mistake." I take a step backward, which causes another spurt of water down my leg. I try to see peripherally if there is anything around I can use as a weapon. Now I wish to God I'd worn the spike-heeled shoes.

"You took him *away* from me!" she cries. "You didn't even *want* him! He was all I had, and now I have nothing!" Her stressed words make me flinch. Even though she hasn't moved, I feel them as lunges.

"Are you talking about Nestor?" I risk another step back. The pain is letting up, and I can think again. Maybe I can make her cry and go limp.

But she gets furious instead. "Don't treat me like I'm *stupid*! Are you saying it's not Nestor's baby in there?" She gestures at June with the knife, slicing the air between us.

Fireworks of rage go off in my head. *No one threatens my baby.* I hear a sound like voices in the distance. Maybe someone heard her yelling and is coming to save us. "I'm not *ever* going to tell anyone whose baby this is!" I shout so loudly her eyes go wide in response. "I made a promise to her father, and I will never break it; even if you *kill* me, I swear I'll never break it and if you do kill me it won't bring Nestor back. Nothing is ever going to bring Nestor back, so everything you're doing now is just going to make your life worse than it already is!"

More water down my leg. It seems like too much. I wonder if something is going wrong.

"What good is a promise you made to a dead guy?" Blanca shouts back. There are tears in her eyes.

I hear the voices again. Or maybe it's musical instruments. It's so faint I can't tell. "Blanca, you need help," I say, calculating the distance between me and the door and wondering how much damage she could do to me before I pull it open. "I understand how you feel. Everyone knows . . . "

"Nobody knows anything!" She reads my mind and steps back toward the door. "We were going to get married right after graduation. I don't have all the other things like you do. I don't have teachers that love me and get me college scholarships. I'm not going to be a writer or a teacher like you are. All I had was Nestor, and you had to ruin that for me. Because you want everything! Acacia was my best friend, and you took her when I needed her the most! Look at you, you whore, in your whore dress! Look in the mirror at yourself! You're disgusting. You're evil . . . " Her voice breaks, and she almost cries. Her muscles loosen, and I think this is the time to try something . . .

Pain seizes me, literally seizes me and bends me double. The flower tumbles out of my hair, showering the floor with petals. I close my eyes and hear the voices clearly now. Recognize them. It's the whales. "No! No! NO!" I scream to June. "Stop it!"

"You're faking that!" Blanca's voice sounds uncertain. "You wouldn't have pains that close together unless you were way into labor."

Oh, my God, she's right. We were warned about the few women who dilated quickly, moving through labor in just a few hours or even an hour. The instructor laughed and said, "Don't count on that happening. It's pretty rare."

Well, I am famous for rare things. Like having a pod of whales coming from the Twilight Zone to assist in my delivery. I hear them clearly now, a harmony of oboes, violins, squealing piccolos.

"Blanca," I manage to gag out. "I've gotta get to the . . . AAAAHHH!" Water pours out of me onto the floor. I'm standing in an inch of water. That's impossible!

"Quit it," she says. "This isn't going to work."

Maybe I should lie down, think about my breathing, take off the dress. I fall on my knees, causing a wave to roll across the bathroom floor and splash up to Blanca's thighs. She doesn't see or feel it. "June, stop it!" I scream. "What are you doing?"

"Who are you talking to?" Blanca's voice is far, far away. "Are you trying to scare me?"

The sprinklers in the ceiling go off. Water bubbles up out of all the sinks. A huge wave hits the door. I try to locate Blanca and can't find her. Is she drowning? The whales are all around me. Their songs, pulsing in my body, ease the pain.

Oh, please, please, June, don't take me to Biscayne Bay to have you!

Then my thoughts aren't human anymore. I'm swimming, following the other whales into deeper water, because it's dangerous to give birth in the shallows. I take a breath and then dive, exhaling down into the cool blue that closes around me like a caress.

13

Deeper, deeper into water so dark and cold it makes me feel calm and still inside. The other whales call at regular intervals, a calming, reassuring pattern. I am in the right place, wherever I am. Cared for by midwives who know exactly what to do.

"She's at ten centimeters already! I want to get a fetal monitor going stat, and somebody get all this . . . dress . . . Cut it off if you have to."

"Did she walk in here? Was she conscious when she came in?"

I feel a contraction that rolls me out of position. The elder females bump me with their heads until I lie in the water correctly. We have done this before in my dreams. I know what to do and feel completely peaceful. It's important not to give in to the urge to breathe.

"Breathe! Breathe! Can you hear me, honey? She's not conscious. I hope . . . "

"She's dripping wet! Where did you find her?"

"Right outside the ER. No one . . . "

"No ID, no purse. She looks under twenty-one."

"Honey? Honey? Honey, can you hear me?"

My mind is split in two. Half of me is rushing on a clattering, rolling cart with lights in my eyes and people all around who are clenched and overexcited. I don't want to be there.

I choose the other half. Deep and cool. The whales are calm about delivery. I arch my spine to ease the pain and feel my lower body expand and contract. The whales sing loudly to encourage me.

"That's Sophie Cooper! Beth Cooper's daughter. Beth is working tonight up on the sixth floor."

"Somebody go get her. We need somebody who can . . . There we go."

Beep. Beep. Beep.

"Okay, good baby. Good mama. Her BP is kind of high. Sophie, can you hear me?"

What has happened to Blanca?

My back is permanently arched. I'm like a bow, and June is a nocked arrow, gathering strength to take flight. When she is ready, she will shoot out, and the others will guide her to the surface.

I'm so happy to be having a baby, I tip back my head and sing.

"Yikes! Did you hear that?"

"Here's Dr. Mendez."

Beep. Beep. Beep.

The invisible man
is waiting
Forbidden fruit in his hands
The roses above wilt
The ground below bleeds asphodel

"Sophie, it's Mom. What's the matter with her?"

"We don't know yet. It's not drugs or alcohol. There's no head trauma. It's like she keeps fainting repeatedly. Some women pass out from the pain, but . . ."

"Sophie! Sophie! Oh, God, why is she like that?"

"Beth, you need to calm down. We don't know where her labor coaches are. We need someone . . . "

"If I had been there when she went into labor . . ."

"We need someone calm to help her through the delivery. Be there for her now, Beth. She might be able to hear everything we say. If you're sorry, be there for her now!"

Humans are never calm. We are always calm, because we have no words to tell ourselves stories with. We just feel what happens. Why would I go back there and listen to that shouting when I can have my baby here? Where everyone knows that birth is natural and everyone is happy for me?

Come to me
like all the Blackbirds before you
the sacred blood has marked you
turn to the South wind with your child
give her to the strongest wind
give the strongest wind to her
A mother is a reed the wind blows through . . .

Beep. Beep. Beep.

"Sophie, can you hear me now? Sophie, if you can hear me, breathe." Dr. Mendez.

The pains are deep and long. They make my body shudder, but it feels right. My companions sing in a frenzy. This is the song for the baby, to encourage her to come.

"We got here as fast as we could." Acacia's voice.

"Yeah, the question is: How did Sophie get here?" That's Joshua. I'm so glad they're here.

"We don't know that." My mother is angry. "Were you

at a dance with her? When's the last time you saw her?"

"We were at the prom, and then . . ."

"At the prom! You took her to a dance when she was in labor? What's wrong with you? Tell the truth. Did you give her something? Did you give her drugs?"

"You must be Sophie's mom. I'm Acacia Williams. This is . . ."

"I know who he is! Dr. Mendez, we have enough going on here without these kids. . . ."

"Beth, these kids are the coaches Sophie requested. If I'm doing anything wrong, it's allowing you to be here when Sophie told me . . . "

Beep. Beep. Beep.

We're coming to the end. I feel a cool, blue bliss, a harmony between my body and the sea around me. I was made to do this. My baby is traveling now, faster and faster. The other whales sing wildly, crazily. I urge my baby with my heart—Launch! Launch!

"Come on, Sophie, come on."

"Squeeze my hand, honey!"

"Help her sit up a little."

"Push, girl! You're almost there."

Beep. Beep. Beep.

Out she explodes in a whoosh of blood, water, and bubbles. The others lunge for her, pushing her to the surface to breathe. I am exhausted, weak, diminished. Some of the females surround me and push, urging me up to get a breath. I feel passive about it. I've done what I had to do; let the others take over.

"Oh, she's beautiful." Acacia.

"But look, look at her . . . " My mother.

"What, you think . . . oh."

Is there something wrong with my baby?

"Sophie? Look, she opened her eyes! Sophie, can you hear me? Can you see me?"

They propel me up through levels of water from the darkest and coldest to layers progressively warmer and brighter. All I want now is to find the baby.

Clunk!

"What was that?"

"Joshua fainted."

"Well, get him out. . . . "

"Sophie, can you look at me? It's Dr. Mendez."

Surfacing, surfacing, surfacing. I break the bright water, breathe in the sunshine, and the beautiful baby whale is there, swimming toward me for her first meal.

I open my eyes and flinch to be back on land, heavy and achy and sore, drenched in salty water. I can't see Joshua. Acacia and my mother are angry. Only Dr. Mendez is happy.

"There we go! Sophie? Are you okay?"

"Yeah." I dimly see nurses in the corner, cleaning and wrapping June. My arms stretch out by themselves. "Is she okay? Where is she?"

"She's perfect," Dr. Mendez says with some kind of overemphasis. "It was you I was worried about."

A nurse brings the little bundle to me and lays it in my arms, and I jump because I was not expecting to see what my daughter is—a beautiful little girl. A beautiful little African-American girl.

My mother walks out of the room.

14

My room is full of sunlight. Beams crisscross June and me, holding us like a net of jewels as she nurses. She's getting drowsy, and she'll drift off for a second, then wake up and suck some more. I don't think she's getting very much, but the nurses say I'll do better with time. When I look down at her and smell her smell, my insides squeeze together with so much love, it hurts me. Sometimes her eyes will look up, but it's more like she's listening than looking. Her eyes are ancient, full of secrets and mysteries. Today, about ten hours old, she looks even more African in her wide-set little features, softly crinkled black hair, eyelashes that look artificially curled. She is still keeping secrets from me.

I insert my finger in her half-closed fist. Her fingers tighten immediately. In one way we know each other completely. In another way we each have mysteries the other one will never find out.

The door opens and my mother comes in, holding a big pink teddy bear and looking scared. My spine stiffens, and June's eyes flick up to mine to see what's wrong.

I cover my breast, pushing June back gently. "If you want to come in here like a normal grandmother and say how beautiful she is, you can stay. But if you're going to start in on what race her father is . . . "

"No, no." I notice the dark circles under her eyes. You can always tell when she hasn't slept, because her face gets all puffy. "I came to tell you. To explain . . . " Her eyes dart around, as if she can't concentrate.

Several minutes of silence follow. I stand June up to help her burp, the way they taught us to do. She makes a cute little sound that makes Mom and me both laugh, but then I force myself to be serious. "The only thing I'll tell you is that Joshua is not the father," I say.

"I know."

"What do you mean, you know!"

"Well . . . " She makes a gesture of erasing things in the air. "I don't know . . . but . . . "

"June's father is white as far as I know, but now I can see he must have . . . "

"No, no, no, Sophie. Not him. It's you."

"What's me?" I glance down, because June is flailing around like she knows the answer.

"Your father." Her eyes plead with me to hurry and understand. "I . . . the reason I . . . I should have told you long ago about Carl but . . . I didn't know what was the right thing to do."

I look down at June's beautiful face. Carl. Carl Wainwright. Suddenly I see. The man I've been picturing who looks sort of like Liam Neeson suddenly changes to Samuel L. Jackson. My father. Me. I look up, stunned, realizing that she failed to tell me something critically important about myself.

"Sophie, I'm sorry. I didn't know what was the right thing to do. I didn't want you to grow up confused."

I'm confused now, so confused that I can't form words. I want to get a mirror, look at my face for the clues I must have missed growing up. I want to think back over my whole life in a different way. Suddenly I'm a stranger to myself.

"We just . . . fell in love." She isn't looking at me anymore. She's talking to the air. "Carl was already married and had a baby. We knew it was wrong. I didn't think I was going to get pregnant."

Who is this talking? Some wayward teen girl from the movies? Not my mom who won't serve a meal without a green vegetable. Not my mom who hasn't gone on a date since I was five years old. Not my mom who frowned on my friendship with Joshua. I wonder if I've been drawn to African-American friends because something inside me was searching. And maybe my mom could see that search, and it scared her.

"We knew it was wrong!" She's begging me to help her, but I can't catch up to where she is. I can't look at this woman I thought I knew and picture her sneaking around with a married man. "We didn't even understand why it happened. It just did."

There. I try to grab onto that. That's something I can understand.

"Did you just do it with him once?" I ask.

"No, no. He was a patient of mine. He had heart problems even then. After he was released he sent me a note about what a good nurse I was. Then he sent me another note a week later, and I realized . . . "

"How old was his child then?" I interrupt. "Was it a boy or a girl?"

"You have two half sisters," she says, understanding the question. "Daniella is two years older than you and goes to the University of Michigan. Juliet is a sophomore at Spanish River. They don't know about you."

I picture myself sneaking into Spanish River High School looking at all the African- American sophomore girls, hoping for a glimpse of my little sister, Juliet.

"We saw each other for about a year. It wasn't tacky, Sophie. I really loved him, and I think he loved me. But he felt guilty. His wife was getting suspicious, and he broke it off. Of course, that was just weeks before I realized I was pregnant with you."

June feels heavy. I look down and see she's fallen asleep, her whole body moving with her deep breaths. I shift her slightly, so her head is supported better.

"Did you tell him?"

She lowers her eyes. "No. I feel guilty about that for your sake, Sophie. Carl had a lot of money. I could have gotten child support, and maybe you wouldn't have had to work and struggle to earn enough for college now. But . . . I didn't want to hurt him or his family, and . . . the selfish thing was, I wanted to prove to myself that I could do everything alone. I felt so helpless at the time. Not telling him made me feel strong. I don't think I can explain it so you can understand it."

This is the one part of the story I do understand. "But you've kept track of him, obviously, or you wouldn't know about his daughters."

Tears stand in her eyes. "Carl, your father, died two years ago. But Mrs. Wainwright is on the library board. She's in the society section all the time. I can't help reading about the family because . . . it's partly your family."

I hardly hear that because I'm wondering, If I were Danielle and Juliet, would I want to find out about my racially mixed half sister, living proof that my dead, saintly father had strayed? Would getting to see a beautiful niece be worth that pain? I don't have the answer for that one yet.

Suddenly my mother starts to cry. "Oh, Sophie, I've made so many mistakes. I've made mistakes on top of mistakes. Can you please come home and at least let me make some of it up to you? We could do it together, take turns with the baby while you go to school and I work. Maybe I could get the night shift. . . . "

June wakes up and starts to cry. Everything comes to a halt as we watch her, heaving and wailing.

That brings in the nurse. She's the one who got me up and helped me with the nursing this morning, but I forget her name. She's African American. Like . . . me.

"Is my sweetie getting tired?" she asks. "Did she finish her breakfast?"

"Yes," I say. "We're all tired."

The nurse laughs. "Hear that, Grandma?" she asks my mother. "Five more minutes, and then I kick you out. Momma needs her rest."

"Okay." Mom has her head down, wiping her eyes.

The nurse takes June out.

"I really do need to rest," I tell her. "It's kind of overwhelming, everything you just told me."

"I understand," she says. "I know."

"I just want to sleep."

"Yes." She sniffs.

"Come back later. Maybe after lunch. We'll talk then. Okay?"

"Okay." She picks up her purse.

"Mom."

"What?"

"It's okay to hug me."

She rushes over and nearly crushes every bone in my body.

When I wake up from my nap, I ask the nurse if she will bring me a mirror. She comes back with a hand mirror, a brush, and some hand lotion on a tray.

"After a baby, all the mothers want to fix up a little," she says.

"Is June okay?" I get nervous when she's away from me, for a variety of reasons. Not just the usual Mommy anxiety, but I'm not totally sure she won't pop off to Biscayne Bay to play with the baby whales. I've known all along that the magic was hers, not mine. It's left me now. My dream during my nap was a plain old dream about running to catch the bus.

"They're checking all her vitals to make sure she's just as perfect as she looks, then she can come back here for another meal. You know in the beginning they like lots of little snacks, all through the day"—she rolls her eyes—"and the night. Want me to brush your hair for you? It's got kind of matted up."

"Yeah," I say softly. "Thank you. What's your name?"

"They call me Kitty. My name is Kitobe." She uses her hands to separate the biggest tangles.

I'm careful not to look up or seem too eager. "Is that African?"

"That's what they tell me." There's a smile in her voice. She is so gentle with my hair. "Swahili. My mother says it means 'precious jewel.' She told me later it was a mistake. She should have looked up the Swahili for 'load of trouble.'"

We both laugh. "Does your mother live here in South Florida?"

"No, my family comes from Cleveland. Most of them are still up there. Bothers me sometimes, but I got recruited to come here, and I love the beach." She's finished with the tangles and picks up the brush, working carefully so it doesn't pull. "Wow, this is curly. You almost don't want to run a brush through this."

"Yeah," I say. "Do you ever get up there to visit them?"

The brushing stops. "You writing a book?"

Busted. "No, I just like to hear about people, and how they do things."

"Well"—the brushing starts up again—"I'm just giving you fair warning, Sophie. I've got a big mouth; and if you encourage me, you'll end up knowing every member of my family, what they like to eat, whether they go to church, what's their favorite song. . . ."

I pick up the mirror and study my face. "Tell me everything," I say.

✯

When Kitty brings June back to me, Dr. Mendez comes along. Dr. Mendez says everything about June is one hundred percent perfect, and she congratulates me on all the things I did right during the pregnancy.

"I'd like you to stay one more night, Sophie," she says. "Your BP is just a little high. I think the delivery was probably pretty hard for you. You were clearly exhausted by the time you got to the hospital. It's amazing that you walked all the way over here from the school."

I realize this is the only conclusion people could have come to. "I don't remember that," I say.

"Well, you must have been a little bit out of your mind, or you would have told your friends to get an ambulance. . ."

"I remember going to the restroom. I thought my water might have broken and then . . . I don't remember anything else."

June makes a sound remarkably like a laugh.

"It's funny what instincts take over, how you must have been half delirious and in pain but you managed to struggle all the way over here . . . "

"In an evening gown," I remind her.

"Oh yes. By the way, that dress got pretty well destroyed in ER. They cut it off you, but they said it was ruined anyway. They said it was soaking wet. In fact, they said you were wet, your hair and everything."

"Weird," I say, wondering how much I owe cousin Tanya for that dress. "Maybe I swam here through the canal system."

"It's a mystery," she says. "But, hey, it's a mystery to me how we can make human beings right in our own bodies. If you live in a world where that can happen, anything can happen."

I realize I really love this woman. And suddenly something in me just melts, gives way. "Her father's not African American," I blurt. "I am." I guess I need to practice saying it so I'll believe it.

Either she's talked to my mother or she's a very calm

lady, because her face hardly reacts. She just shrugs. "We're all mixed, Sophie. The races we think we are, are just an illusion."

I think that's a pretty cool statement, one I'll want to remember later. In a way she's right. I know I'm exactly the same person I was before my mom told me, but in another way, I'm not. It's like that dream where you find a secret room in your house that's so full of treasures, you don't know where to look first.

An hour later I get my next practice session when Joshua and Acacia come to visit. You can feel the tension between them as Joshua puts a basket of lilacs next to Mom's teddy bear.

Acacia comes up to me and looks only at June, who is sleeping in the crook of my arm. "She's beautiful, Sophie," she says in an emotional voice.

I put my hand on her arm, make her look at me. "Acacia," I say. "Joshua is not the father of this baby. I swear to you on June's life."

Joshua remains at the foot of the bed, hands in pockets, head down. I see now he's very angry. "My word not good enough," he hisses under his breath.

Acacia's eyes search mine. "But who else would you be protecting?"

"That's my business," I say. "But I found out something this morning, and I need to tell somebody. My mother told me I'm biracial. I never had a clue. That's why June looks African American, not because of who her father is. Because of who my father is."

Well, I've found a real attention getter for cocktail parties. Joshua's head snaps up, and he does what Acacia is now doing: stares at me as if I'm a specimen under a microscope.

"Naw!" he says, then cocks his head the other way. "Yeah?"

"I can see it," Acacia says. "Don't look at her color. Look

at her features, Joshua. Look at her eyes."

"Naw!" he says. He comes in closer, squints at me in a way that cracks me up. "Naw!"

"Yes, Joshua." I giggle uncontrollably. "I'm a sistah."

This makes us all laugh hysterically for some reason, maybe to let out the tension. June wakes up, but she settles down again.

"Your mother never told you?" Acacia says. "That's wrong, Sophie. It's part of your heritage."

"Oh, no!" Joshua puts his hands over his ears. "Here it comes. The black history lecture. The meaning of Kwaanza . . . "

"Shut up." Acacia laughs. "But it's true. I can't even imagine what Sophie is feeling right now."

"Neither can Sophie," I say. "I think if June had looked . . . more like me, my mother would never have told me."

"That's wrong," Acacia says. She looks at Joshua. "I guess I owe you an apology."

He folds his arms and wriggles up to full height. "Well, I guess you do!"

"I'm sorry, baby. I went the wrong way."

"Well, next time don't doubt my word." He puts his nose up in the air.

"Okay, Josh, don't milk it," I say.

"Can I pick her up?" Acacia asks in a voice like a little girl's.

"Sure," I say.

She scoops up June like a pro, rocking her and looking deep into her face. "Oh, you're so pretty, Miss June Baby. Oh, yes, you are."

"Oh, God!" Joshua cries. "I think I just saw my whole life flash before me!"

I turn to laugh at him, and when I turn back, I see tears pouring out of Acacia's eyes. I had forgotten.

129

"Oh, honey," I say. "You'll have your own. You will."

"After we finish college," Joshua says hurriedly.

Acacia struggles for control. June flails, maybe looking for me. "You arrogant man!" Acacia says to Joshua. "I haven't even decided if you're good enough to be the father of my babies! Sophie, I'm sorry; just for a minute, I . . . "

"Of course you did," I say. "Listen, you're going to get so much practice babysitting, you'll feel as if she is yours."

"You hear that, Miss June?" Acacia goes back to her baby voice. "Your auntie will teach you how to shop and paint your itty-bitty nails . . . "

"Thank God it's not a boy!" Joshua says. "Listen, Sophie, what happened when you went into labor?"

I reach for June, stalling for time. "What do you mean?"

"I mean, where were you? How'd you get here? What happened with Blanca?"

I shiver. "Blanca?"

"How would she know about that?" Acacia says. She turns to me. "Blanca had some kind of . . . breakdown at the prom. They found her in the bathroom, waving a knife and screaming. She . . . you know the whole thing about Nestor . . . She never got over it. She should have had counseling when he died."

"Waving a knife?" I say softly.

"She was raving on about you," Joshua says. "Calling you a witch and talking about how you sent a flock of birds after her."

"Birds?" I make the mistake of asking June, but then I look up quickly.

"Blackbirds," Acacia says. "She said you lured her into the bathroom and then called on hundreds of blackbirds to come out and attack her."

"We could hear her screaming all the way back in the

gym, even with the music playing." Joshua picks up the story. "Everybody went running down there—I thought it might be you going into labor—and they opened the bathroom door and she was stabbing at the air, stabbing at the birds that weren't there; and then Coach Ferguson grabbed her, and she practically stabbed him; and all the time she was hollering about you and your witchcraft."

"It was frightening," Acacia says. "I never saw anybody completely out of their mind like that. They took her off to some hospital . . . Happy Valley or some scary name like that."

"Coral Hills," Joshua says. "They gave her the Baker Act. Didn't even wait for her mom to come."

"Then we finally realized you were missing," Acacia says. "And we . . . everyone panicked because she had a knife and she'd been talking about you. They started searching the school for . . . "

Joshua interrupts. "And then your doctor called the school to find us and said you had gotten to the hospital somehow. . ."

"Dr. Mendez says I must have walked." That's my story, and I'm sticking to it. I give June a little look, though. I don't get the part about the blackbirds. I thought my witch-child was a whale specialist.

Joshua is looking at me a little funny. He knows me well enough to know when I'm fudging on the truth. Or it could be that by now he has enough pieces of the puzzle to realize who the father really is. "I guess the important thing is that you got here somehow, and the baby is okay."

"You know the first thing Joshua said when we found out you were here in the hospital?" Acacia's eyes twinkle.

"Uh-uh!" he says.

"What?" I ask.

"He said, 'Thank God she didn't do it in that rented

limo!'" She throws him a triumphant look.

"Well," he giggles. "They charge extra for getting placenta on the seats and stuff!"

When they leave, they're holding hands.

"That's your aunt and uncle," I tell June.

15

Mrs. Chanate walks into my room. At first I think I'm dreaming, because I had fallen asleep with June in the crook of my arm. I don't even know what time of day it is. The room is full of grayish violet light. It could be twilight. It could be dawn.

"May I come?" she asks from the doorway.

"Of course." I sit up, repositioning June, so Mrs. Chanate can see her granddaughter's face.

She shows me the flowers she has brought: wildflowers in a water glass. She has trouble fitting them on my table crowded with formal arrangements that suddenly look weird and artificial. She walks in close. Her eyes, on the baby, are steady and peaceful. "A girl," she says.

"Yes." I'm surprised there's no comment on June's color. "Her name is June."

"Ahhh . . . May I hold her?"

I have this crazy, fleeting feeling she will grab June and spirit her away, but I push it down. "Of course."

Mrs. Chanate scoops her up expertly (I still feel awkward holding her) and coos into her face. "June," she says. "Hello,

June." She studies the baby for a long moment, as if memorizing her, then hands her back. "Thank you," she says.

There's a pause, then we both try to speak at once. "You go," I tell her.

"I know you want to keep it a secret about Nestor," she says.

"Maybe not anymore."

"Did you make a promise to him?"

"Yes. Because he was in love with Blanca, and he didn't want to hurt her."

"He had no future with her," she says firmly. "But you're right, he thought he did."

"He must have told you all about . . . him and me." I shift June away from my breast, because she's acting as if she wants to clamp on, and I need to concentrate.

"No, no, he didn't tell me anything. I didn't know he ever even took you out."

"He didn't exactly. It was sort of . . . "

She holds up her hand. "Protect your privacy, Sophie. It's the most powerful thing you have. It isn't important how it happened. Nestor is gone now . . . " She pauses, and I realize she is waiting for an urge to cry to pass. "And Blanca . . . Blanca has never been right. . . . She is unbalanced. I don't know if any of those doctors even know how to balance her. So you have made a promise of secrecy that . . . doesn't matter anymore." She turns her face away.

She is so composed, and yet I get the sense that she's full of emotion at the same time. I've never known anyone like her, except maybe her son. "I'm realizing how important it is for June to . . . know where she came from."

She smiles. "More than you know."

I don't know what that means, but I stumble on. "So now, if you will, Mrs. Chanate, I want you to be a part of June's life and teach her about Cuban culture."

She smiles again. "Not Cuban."

I'm lost. I'm almost positive Nestor and Joshua both told me that Nestor's parents came to the U.S. from Cuba as children.

"My ancestors have lived in Cuba for a long time," she says. "The same with Nestor's father. But our homeland, our true culture is right here." Her finger stabs at the floor. "We are Tequesta."

Shivers start up in my stomach. "Like the Miami Circle people? But I thought there were no more Tequestas. I thought the settlers wiped them out."

"No. They put our ancestors on a boat. A boat to Cuba."

The light in the room shifts from lavender to blood-red. It must be dawn. June is getting ready to cry, so I cuddle her, pressing my face into hers. I've already learned she likes that.

"My ancestors were determined that our way of life would not be destroyed. We refused to let our culture die a slow death. We learned Spanish, pretended to mix in; but we kept our clan names, never married outside, practiced our religion in secret. We Tequesta are alive and well, all over Cuba and other places. Like here. We are known only to each other. That is why I wanted to come to you, Sophie. Your baby is part Tequesta, and it is important for me to tell you and to welcome you into our clan."

She pauses to adjust the clip that holds her hair. She has the same kind of hair as Nestor, the same peaceful, steady eyes. I look down at my mysterious child, think of all the magical things that are hidden inside her.

"My late husband, Mr. Chanate, was of the blackbird clan," she says. "Chanate means 'blackbird.'"

My body jerks involuntarily. I think of Blanca, screaming that I had sent blackbirds to attack her.

"Nestor has his father's last name, because in America the baby must take the father's name. But the clan passes down through the mother. Because you are not an Indian, June is really a part of my clan. My name is Ballena."

I already know, although I don't speak Spanish. "The whale clan."

She stands up taller. "Yes. The Ballena are a prestigious clan. The whale is the most sacred animal of all to the Tequesta. We hunted the whales . . . "

"Off Biscayne Bay."

"Yes."

"The hunters jumped on the whale's backs and speared them."

She frowns gently. "That's what I've been told. . . . Did you . . . "

"Your people had the power to turn themselves into whales, too. So you could learn all their secrets." I'm so relieved, it feels like exhaustion.

"That's the legend, but . . . "

"And somehow they could travel from one place to another, just like that." I snap my fingers.

"You couldn't have learned this in school. I was taught these things by my mother."

June is getting really cranky. I put her up over my shoulder. "I was taught these things by my daughter."

June burps, out of character for the powerful shaman that she is. We both laugh.

"There are things I would like to be able to teach you and the baby," Mrs. Chanate says. "There are ceremonies that have always been performed. Nestor thought it was all nonsense. He was a product of this culture, but . . . "

"Don't worry," I say. "I've been learning for the past nine months that June is special. She'll . . . we'll need to know everything you have to teach us."

The only other dance I ever went to, besides the prom, was

Homecoming. Joshua made me do it, insisting that if I acted more sociable, suddenly I'd be like Cinderella at the ball, and my whole life would change. People like Joshua, who have never been shy, don't understand people like me: the wall that goes up in your brain, blocking out all your coherent thoughts, the flood of memories of all the times you've tried to approach other kids and they've snubbed you, or worse. The knowledge that you are sweating, blushing, or, like I was that night, shaking.

I stood against the wall in my Kmart dress printed with violets—a literal wallflower—for the whole night, staring at the people, even the most hopeless-looking geeks, who were somehow able to find partners and get up and dance.

Acacia had a different boyfriend back then, whom she clung to all night. Likewise, Blanca and Nestor were inseparable. They looked beautiful together, and I realize now I was staring at him a lot. The contrast between his starched tuxedo and the waterfall of wild, black hair down his back, his endless composure, the way his spine swayed in the direction his feet were about to step so that Blanca, with her hand on his waist, could follow his intent.

Joshua pried me off the wall for a couple of lame dances, but I stepped all over his feet, terrified that people were looking at me. After a while, he gave up on me and left me to my wall.

As I often do when I'm really upset, I turned to my imagination and started thinking about Persephone. Mr. Kissanis had just told us the myth, and I loved it for some reason. Standing on the dance floor, I suddenly knew why. My only hope was some kind of abduction. A boy would have to fall in love with me from afar and drag me, kicking and screaming, into a relationship. Drag me away from my mother, whom I knew already expected to live with me forever, because she had no one else. Feed me pomegranates and teach me all the wonderful things that happen in the dark.

Somewhere in the middle of this fantasy, I noticed Joshua whispering to Nestor, and everything in my stomach crowded into my throat. Blanca was nowhere in sight. Nestor glanced at me as Joshua talked, checking out the pathetic friend who couldn't attract boys. Then he looked toward the exit that leads to the restroom and gave a nervous answer back to Joshua. Joshua leaned in close and whispered some kind of long speech. When Joshua goes to work on you, you might as well give in. Nestor did. He started walking toward me, still throwing terrified glances at the exit.

It seems to take him hours to get to me. If only a fissure would open up in the ground and take me in. "Hi, wanna dance?" he says to the exit sign.

"No, thanks." I decide it's time to go home, even if I have to walk.

My refusal completely shifts his gears. He forgets to watch for Blanca and stares at me incredulously. "Say what?"

I laugh at him. All the boys on the basketball team try to "talk black," and Nestor doesn't pull it off very well. "I'd rather not dance," I say. "It's nothing personal."

He blinks at me a few times and grabs my hand. "I think you meant 'yes,'" he says, pulling me out to the floor, and my abduction begins.

At some point as we are dancing, I see that Blanca has come back from the bathroom and is staring at us with so much rage, it feels like heat on my back.

"She thinks she owns me," Nestor comments, swinging me around gracefully. I dance well with him, because I've studied him so much. "You're pretty, you know that? What are you, some kind of honor student?"

I guess he's trying to explain to himself why he never noticed me before.

After our dance Nestor throws Joshua a "thanks a lot"

look and goes over to Blanca. She makes for the exit. He follows. I return to my wall to catch up on my trembling. Joshua is dancing with a cheerleader, oblivious to the disasters he has set in motion.

Minutes later Nestor comes back, alone. He looks a little disheveled. He looks at Joshua one more time and then walks back to me. "You wanna dance again?" he asks. "I got no date."

"How could I refuse such a gracious offer?" I say.

He looks startled that such a long sentence could come out of me. "Come on." He holds out his hand. "It's a dance. We're supposed to be having fun."

I could taste the pomegranate seeds in my mouth.

It gets late. Nestor and I dance a lot. Blanca's friends, especially Acacia, frown at us from time to time. Joshua has apparently fallen in love with the cheerleader and asks Nestor if he will drive me home. With his usual poetics Nestor says, "Why not, I'm screwed anyway."

We drive. I try to make conversation to control my shaking. "Do you love Blanca?"

He makes a scrunchy face at this question. "I'd like to marry her. She needs somebody to take care of her, and I'm good at that. My mom is against it, though. She's got some kind of crazy ideas about tradition or something."

"You'd marry someone just because they need you?"

He gives me the longest look he can without going off the road. "How come you don't have a boyfriend?"

I feel myself blush. "That's a rude question."

He laughs. "I thought that's the game we were playing, honey."

"No! You're asking me to tell you what I think is wrong with me because boys aren't attracted to me. It's like if you messed up a play on the court and somebody asked you why you did that."

"So? The coach does that all the time. Can I tell you

something? I mean, I don't know you, but you're Joshua's friend, so you must be pretty cool. I can see that you're gorgeous. I had fun with you tonight. If you don't have a boyfriend, it's because you don't try."

I sigh. "That's what Joshua says. I don't know how to try, though, Nestor. I don't know what to try."

"Smile. Say hello." He smiles. "If someone asks you to dance, don't say 'no'".

"You didn't want to dance with me."

His eyes flick over. "I never do anything I don't want to do."

I let a few seconds pass. "I'm the opposite," I say. "I never do anything I want to do."

The eyes flick again. "What do you want to do right now?"

He knows a place to park, of course. He and Blanca have probably parked there a hundred times. I tell myself I'll just kiss him and that will be it. Persephone had to reach for that one, really beautiful flower. At first his kisses are like little questions. I realize you don't have to be in love if you're with someone beautiful, and you're hungry and lonely, and you think it's your only chance. He keeps his hands down at his sides until I touch him. Then this sort of growl comes out of his throat, and his fingers tangle in my hair, and the ground beneath us opens up.

High noon. Soon my mother will come in, hoping to take me home. Mike and Reid think the same thing. I can't make a decision, because my mind is so full of other things. Who I am. Who Nestor was. Who June is. I push my lunch tray away and stare at the table in front of me crowded with flowers and toys. The only thing I know for sure is that June will have lots of babysitters.

My mother comes in, chewing on her lip. Reading her

face, I know what I must have looked like hugging the wall at that dance, praying someone would pick me. She has brought another oversized toy for June, this time a giraffe. I think how long it's going to take to load all this stuff in a car.

"I'm going to live with Mike and Reid, Mom."

The giraffe sags in her arm. "I know you're angry with me right now."

"No. I'm not angry. What would I be angry with you for? Everything you did, I did. You loved somebody who was unavailable. You tried to keep a secret out of honor."

"Yes, yes!" She pleads. "Then why . . . "

"Because I want to keep on being like you. You raised me all by yourself. You went to school. You worked. That's the only reason I believe I can do it, Mom. Because I saw you do it every single day."

"But I had to! My parents wouldn't help me."

"They did you a favor. Like I'm doing now. Like we'll have to do for June someday. Women have to know they can take care of themselves. That's the best thing you ever gave me. Don't try to take it away now."

"But the baby . . . " she says. "I was hoping . . . "

"I'm only three blocks away. You'll get to babysit a lot. I'm going to have one heck of a schedule to juggle."

"Okay."

I've never heard her back down so easily. Is it because she knows in her heart this is the right thing or because this is the first time I've talked to her like a fellow adult and not a whiny kid?

"Let's take a trip together next summer," I say. "To celebrate me finishing my first year of college. We'll take June to Disney World or something."

She's relaxing more and more. I have a lot to thank Mr. Kissanis for. Without the myth I wouldn't have thought of giving my mom her own season with the baby.

In the next few minutes, the room fills up with people. Mike and Reid come in, both very shy, but Reid gives me the hugest hug when he finds out I'm his live-in babysitter for the next four years. Joshua and Acacia come in, and a nurse tells them they're getting June ready and if they want to they can start loading my stuff in the car.

The group breaks into gender stereotypes as the men all start loading their arms with plants and toys and head down to the parking lot.

They bring in June and my ceremonial wheelchair. Acacia has brought a dress for June's first day in the real world. It's over the top, something Barbie would wear to a formal wedding, but I help Acacia torture June into it. I know I have to share this baby with all the women who need her. When she's dressed, I struggle to get out of bed.

"Let me hold her," says Acacia.

"Let me help you," says my mother.

I let them.

16

It's June twenty-first, the summer solstice, the most sacred day in the Tequesta calendar. We have gathered on the north shore of Biscayne Bay for a ceremony Mrs. Chanate says is important in June's life. Mrs. Chanate is presenting my daughter to the winds. In the old days it would have happened the day she was born, but it takes us modern people longer to organize things.

I stand between the grandmothers in my sunflower dress, reading from the poem June dictated to me.

Come to me
on the day of fire
the Day of the Sun
stand in the circle of grandmothers
lift your child to the fourfold embrace

A mother is a reed the wind blows through
A mother is a reed the wind blows through

Mrs. Chanate lifts June high over her head, so the east wind can see her. Even though the day has been hot and still, a breeze begins to blow.

Come to me
at first light
While the East wind teases the sea

Behind us sits our audience. Joshua and Acacia, Mike and Reid. Acacia has catered the event. Perrier Jouet for her and Joshua, Diet Coke for my mom, Gatorade for Mike and Reid, and bottled water for Mrs. Chanate and me. Everyone agreed on cake. I asked for the Carvel ice-cream cake that's shaped like a whale. Mrs. Chanate laughed when she saw it.

Mrs. Chanate turns north, toward the condos of Aventura. I read:

While the North wind shadows our secrets

I think about my secrets and Acacia's secrets and my mother's secrets and the secret Tequesta people of Cuba, living in exile. I used to think keeping secrets was a kind of lying. Now I see it's a way of protecting something until it's ready to be born.

Mrs. Chanate faces west, toward Miami.

While the West wind comforts our dead

I look over our guests and think about the ones who should be there. Nestor. My father. I promise myself I will keep them alive for June, so she'll never feel like I did, that a piece of myself was missing.

Mrs. Chanate turns south, toward the bay. The wind blows hard, whipping my dress like a flag. The three of us wade into the water. Mrs. Chanate holds my baby over the place where her ancestors hunted.

Come to me
like all the Chanates before you
the sacred blood of the Ballenas has marked you
turn to the south wind with your child
give her the strongest wind
give the strongest wind to her

This is the only part of the ceremony that frightens me. Seeing Mrs. Chanate hold June over the water. I'm afraid my baby will disappear and join the whales, but it's been two weeks, and June has behaved like a perfectly normal baby. Maybe she was only able to do magic when she had my body to use as an amplifier. Maybe now she has to wait for her grandmother to train her before she can reclaim her power.

June is looking down at the bright surface of Biscayne Bay. The reflected sun makes diamonds on her face. Even if she can't do her magic anymore, I know she is seeing beyond the surface, knowing that everything really valuable is hidden in the depths.

We all chant the last lines together:

A mother is a reed the wind blows through
A mother is a reed the wind blows through